FORBIDDEN BOOK 1

KATHI S. BARTON

This is a work of fiction. Names, characters, places, and incidents are products of the author's imagination or are used fictitiously and are not to be construed as real. Any resemblance to actual events, locations, organizations, or persons, living or dead, is entirely coincidental.

World Castle Publishing, LLC
Pensacola, Florida
Copyright © Kathi S. Barton 2017
Paperback ISBN: 9781629895536
eBook ISBN: 9781629895543
First Edition World Castle Publishing, LLC, March 20, 2017
http://www.worldcastlepublishing.com
Licensing Notes
Cover: Karen Fuller
Editor: Maxine Bringenberg

CHAPTER 1

His wife had left him. Jake wasn't sure how he felt about it, but she was gone, that was a sure thing. And she'd taken everything; not just her things, but every stick of furniture in the house. He definitely wasn't unhappy about that. Jake thought his wife had horrific taste in all manners of style.

Jake figured that he should have seen it coming; he'd been seeing little signs that she wasn't happy with him. Hell, he wasn't happy with himself. But he had been trying his best to make her happy. Okay, maybe not happy, but at least make her life with him tolerable. Carol wasn't really the nicest person in the world, nor did she tolerate fools easily. Well, not at all, and he thought she had it in her head that he was the biggest fool of them all.

Jake Winslow had married his high school...Jake wasn't sure she was his girlfriend or his sweetheart, but he did marry

5

her when he'd been fresh out of high school. She'd told him, several times during his senior year, that if he didn't marry her by the time he left for college, she'd not be around when he returned. Jake was never sure why he did it—he certainly didn't love her—but she was the only woman he'd had sex with. He supposed he'd been led by his dick, as most men were.

His parents had made him marry her. Jake wasn't sure why that thought had entered his head after all these years, but he knew as surely as he was standing in his empty house that they'd made him. He hadn't wanted to, not at all. If she'd not been there when he returned, then she'd just be gone. Pressure from his father and whining from his mother had made him do it. He was sure of that.

So, fresh from his graduation he asked her to marry him, and of course she'd said yes. And the week before he left for college, they were married...right there on her parents' front lawn. His parents had decided not to come to the quick wedding... something about contracts and money to be made. Money; he knew this was a huge factor in his father's life. Jake had wished so many times over the last ten years that he'd just gone off to college and never returned. He might have but for the one person in his life that he loved more than he did himself—his grandma, Jenna Beck Winslow.

As he made his way around the house, empty of even any foodstuffs, he thought of the things he'd have to do now. File for divorce, he supposed. Since she'd left him, he figured he'd be safe in betting that she'd gotten all she wanted from him. There really wasn't much left for her to take anyway. He'd taken care of most of his property and stocks when she refused to sign a pre-nup as his grandma had suggested. The rest; well, he'd hidden that away as well.

This house was in his grandma's name. As were the deeds to the two buildings that he had downtown, other holdings in deals, as well as a few other things that Grandma and he held together. He'd done most of the hiding of assets several years ago, right after Carol had nearly gotten them in trouble with the IRS for not filing their taxes as she said she'd been doing. It had taken him nearly four months of working a lot of overtime and taking cases he didn't like to pay back his grandma the money she'd generously lent him. Paying Grandma back had been the one argument he'd won with Carol. After that, he changed a lot of things.

As he stood in the kitchen, he thought of the last fight that they'd had in this room not three nights ago. He'd been working late, again, and had come in this room to fix something to tide him over until breakfast. Carol had come in and started on him about money.

"The checking account is empty." He didn't even bother looking at her. He knew it was. He'd emptied it when he'd noticed her spending had gotten out of hand. "I need you to put something in the account so that I can go to the mall tomorrow. Borrow it from that old woman again if you have to, but there has to be money in the account when I need to buy something. I've been invited to go to the mall with some of the girls from the country club. You know how important it is to me to keep up appearances, and besides, some of my favorite stores are running a sale. That requires money in the bank, because, in case you didn't notice, the credit cards aren't working either."

"I'm not borrowing money from my grandma again. She's been kind enough to us. And the credit cards aren't working because I canceled them. All of them." She asked him why he'd do that. "Because, as I have told you several times over the last six months, there isn't that kind of money coming in to cover even the minimum payment the way you spend money. You have to stop using them for every little thing you want. I've told you that. And since you can't even do that, then I've taken control of them out of your hands."

He didn't say *for now*, because Jake knew that she'd only continue to spend the money as if there were no limits. Charging things like ugly furniture that no one sat on. Dresses that would still have the tags on them when she donated them to some cause that the other sheep were into. And she'd go to restaurants and pay for everyone's meals even though she didn't like them any better than she did him. No, Jake had thought, she wasn't getting any more ways to spend money.

She had growled at him, something he'd only just noticed that he thought was juvenile. "I don't know why you're doing this to me, but I want you to know that I do not care for it. You make enough money for me to spend a few bucks now and again, Jake. Fix this." He told her he had. Just not the way she wanted. "I don't care what you do, but I'm going to the mall in the morning and I'm going to use those cards. I would suggest that if you don't want me going to jail, because I will throw the fit of all fits, then you'd better make this right."

He'd finished making his sandwich and sat down at the table. Even before he could pick up his dinner of cold roast beef on a hotdog bun, all he could find, she swiped it from the table and onto the floor. He hadn't wanted to get into it with her, but she had left him no choice. Jake knew that shouting at her would get him nothing but a headache. Carol was ten times more stubborn than any other person he knew. He'd looked at her as she stood before him with a self-satisfied smirk on her face.

"Why are you like this? Why do you treat me as if I'm nothing more than a way for you to have the things you want?" She said nothing but stared at him, tapping her foot as she'd done so many times in the past. Well, he wasn't going to give in this time, no matter what she said or did. "I'm not going to put money in the bank so you can spend it on foolish things. Nor am I going to reinstate the credit cards so that you can run the limit to the max again. I got them paid off now, and there is no reason for you to—"

"If you paid them off, then there no reason whatsoever that I can't have them back, Jake. There are plenty of things I can buy now. The entire house could use a once over. Things are stale here. Give the cards to me and I will buy you something nice for that nasty office you work in." He just stared at her after telling her to leave his office alone. "Jake, I'm not kidding you. If you don't give me those cards, I'm going to leave you. Then what will you do? I should have the things I want. I did marry you."

"I married you as well, Carol. And you're going to put us in the poor house with your total disregard to money and how it's made. I purchased you this overpriced house that I didn't want and the car that you seldom drive. You promised me then that you'd curb your spending. I can't keep working like this so that you can toss our money away like you have no respect for how hard I work for it." She simply put out her hand as if he was just going to turn them over. "I'm done. I'm not going to do this with you again."

When she left him there, he stood to clean up his mess. He wasn't surprised when he heard the door to the bedroom slam, nor did he react when he heard her screaming. It was her way, he supposed, to make sure that everyone, including the neighbors, knew when she was displeased. They were probably used to it by now; he certainly was.

Jake, as he had done for a while now, had gone to one of the spare bedrooms to sleep. He even went so far as to lock the door, and then put the dresser in front of it. He didn't think that she'd harm him, but he didn't want to take the chance that she'd come in and try to take whatever she found in his wallet. The cards, like a great many things he didn't want her to have, were in the safe at his grandma's home.

And now here he was in his home with no wife, no tables and chairs, and probably not a single thing he could sleep on. Moving to the living room now he saw that she'd left him a nice note. The walls of this room were smeared with what he could only surmise was her last calling card. The note was written in spray paint all over the walls and over the fireplace. He, in a sort of disjointed way, thought about the amount of effort she'd taken to do this when he couldn't even get her to clean up after herself in the bath.

Dear deadbeat, I have found that I can no longer live under the rules that you've put me under. Good riddance.

Jake grinned and wished this other man, if there was

another one, all the luck in the world. He was going to need it, and a fat bank account. Jake was sure that even if the man had an endless supply of money it would never be enough for Carol. He pulled out his cell phone and called the only woman he'd ever loved. His mom hadn't ever meant as much to him as his grandma did, and he doubted if she ever would.

"Carol left me." She told him good. "Yeah, I figured you'd say that. She took everything too. I'm pretty sure if there was a mouse in the house, he'd be starved by morning. I don't have a pot to even piss in now, and oddly enough, I don't really care. And when I was in my bedroom a little while ago, I noticed that she fixed my suits for me too. They're cut to shreds."

"She was a dreadful child, and she didn't improve when she became an adult. I blame that on her parents, because they're not much better. Frightful people." He laughed as he sat on the stairs. "Why don't you come here tonight? You and I will get drunk, eat some dinner, and have a good laugh over her. I don't suppose she left you for another man, did she? That poor bastard."

"I don't know. I think if there were a man out there that could keep up with her spending, he'd be sorry before now. Carol was mad about the credit cards." He looked at the wall and repeated what Carol had written there. "And on a good note, I no longer have to cover up the couch when I want to sit on it...if I had a couch. I have never in all my life known a woman who had a negative sense of style like Carol has. And if there is another man, I'm betting he'll have no idea what he's getting himself into until it's too late."

"Oh well, not your problem any longer, I'm thrilled to say.

The girl needed to have left you a long time ago." He agreed with his grandma. "Come over here and we'll celebrate. I'll have Bonny freshen your room up and we'll have some fun. Lord knows you deserve it after ten years of hell."

"I'm exhausted, Grandma, and don't think I have the energy to drive." She asked him what he was going to sleep on, the floor? "I have no idea, but I'm just too tired to go out tonight. I'll come over tomorrow and we'll plot. I know I have to file for divorce now; I'm done with her. And hire someone good to take the case. I think her parents will want me to give her everything despite how much she already took."

"I'll talk to my attorney. He never cared for Carol anyway after all the stories I've told him. He'd more than likely do it for free." Jake laughed. "Come over, darling. I want to see you."

"I really can't. I'm not sure I have the energy to even drive there. I'll just find some blankets—I think there are a couple in my car—and spread them out on the floor. I'm too tired to care if I have a lot of comforts or not." He walked to the door to go to his car even as he continued. "Tomorrow is Saturday. I'll come over in the morning and have breakfast with you. One thing that's good about this is that I don't have to work myself to death to pay for her shit." Jake looked around and shuddered.

The couch in this room had been a bright green paisley. The chair a solid green that was almost blue green in color. The pillows had been plaid. He had avoided looking at the drapes, a deep blood red color that was a combination of squares and some sort of squidgy design that had made him seasick. Every room in the house was like that, brightly overdone and full of so many patterns that he never could figure out what she'd been going for.

"I'm so glad that you're looking at this as a positive thing. She was a mess and we both knew it. All right, go to sleep and I'll see you first thing in the morning. I'll have Cook make your favorites. Even bacon." He laughed when she did. His grandma loved bacon more than he did. "I love you, Jake. Take care tonight."

"I will."

As he spread out the blanket he'd unearthed from the trunk of his car, he thought of what order things had to go in now that he was alone. The house would have to go. But even as he lay down on the floor with the fireplace roaring out at him, he knew that he'd keep it. It was his after all, and Carol would be jealous that he had it.

As he lay there, thinking of his life thus far, all he could feel was relieved. He was free. For the first time in his adult life, Jake was free. Rolling to his back, he could see his life as it had played out before him. From the first moment he'd seen Carol, he knew that she wasn't for him. There was just something so.... While he didn't think she was evil, he'd never felt particularly safe around her. Then after Jake had done a little investigating, he knew better than to piss her off.

Carol had set her sights on him for a reason that he just couldn't understand. His family had money, that was true, but he didn't have anything that he could claim as his own. At least not back then. He'd not even gotten a new car for graduation as she had. The car he drove was a beater that his grandma had helped him get for running around campus, and he used a four-year-old computer. Plus, he had received a scholarship to one of the most prestigious colleges in the country. Jake had worked really hard for that.

After he and Carol had been married for about a month, she started coming to him about money. She needed this or that. As a student paying rent for a house while he was in college, there wasn't enough money in the account for him to buy books and her things. She'd never let him live down the fact that he'd made her suffer by not having any money all the time. But when he'd been taken in by a very good firm, Jake thought he'd more than made up for her *suffering*.

Jake didn't understand most of the things that she purchased, either. Who needed ten pair of shoes when you could only wear one at a time? And why did she need a new coat for every season? What was wrong with the one that she had in her closet? Most of the time he went without one just so she'd be happy. But she was never happy, nor was she ever satisfied, he'd just realized. No matter what he did or sacrificed for her, it was never enough.

After he'd gotten out of school there were plenty of offers for him to look over. He'd been looking for stability, a good income, and a place he could like going to work for daily. A good firm that he could be proud to work for, and one that, someday, he'd be able to be a partner with. Carol had had a different outlook on his job prospects. She wanted location. An address that said she had money, or at least the appearance of it.

There were questions that she had about where they'd live. How they'd live was questioned too, things such as servants, lawn service, and even limo rides. Where the closest mall was.

Was there a country club membership involved? Would she be a part of the firm's family as well, such as receiving invites to the partners' homes? And she expected parties and shopping sprees.

"I don't think we should care about that so much just yet." Carol had asked him what she should be caring about then. "Well, schools for our children. Where we might find the safest neighborhoods. And how quickly I can climb the corporate ladder. Mostly I think we should pay off some of our debt that we got while I was in college, and then save for a smaller house at first."

"No, I don't want that at all. The bills? Those are your problem, not mine. You could have worked while going to college, and if you had, you'd not owe so much. Jake, if I'm going to be a lawyer's wife, then I can expect things to go my way for a change. I catered to your needs enough while you were off studying." She made it sound as if he'd not been working hard at his classes and had fucked around. Jake wondered even then if she realized how much things went her way now. "We'll find us a house that I want, then you can work from there if you'd like. But I deserve a nice home, bigger than my daddy's."

He was never sure how she was going to make that work. Nine firms wanted him to come and work for them, two of them in another state. But Carol had not only found her a house she could tolerate—her words to him when they moved in—but she also got a house much larger than they needed. She called it their starter house, whatever the hell that meant. Lucky for them, or at least him, it wasn't far from his grandma's, and he could go see her whenever he wished.

Jake realized that he wasn't going to get any sleep with his mind so busy, so he pulled out the laptop from his briefcase and turned it on. As he searched for things to fill his home, he found himself looking on sites for furniture that his wife might have wanted. So, with a huge smile, he put in searches for things that he might like. By the time the sun was coming up, not only had Jake filled two rooms of the house, but he'd found that he was having fun. By the time he made his way to his grandma's house, he was actually giddy with contentment.

~~~

Carol smiled when she thought of her husband. In a few days she'd call him, find out how much he was suffering, and then tell him that she'd take him back. But under her terms. There would be no more of his cutting off her spending. It was her right to spend as much money as she wished, and he should have realized that before now. Sitting on the large bed that had come with the hotel she'd set up for herself, Carol knew it was just a matter of time before he'd come to his senses. Jake was a nice man, but nice men finished last. Carol was going to have to teach him that lesson sooner or later.

"Carol, do you think this is the smartest move you can make right now with Jake? I mean, he is due for his annual bonus, you told me. Had you waited for that, you could have set yourself up nicely instead of borrowing from me to finance this idea you have." Carol told her mother that it was in the bag. "If you say so. I think he might like you being gone. Your father and I certainly are glad to have you gone from our house."

"What a thing to say to me, Mother. You have always been so mean to me. Why is that? I think you're just jealous, aren't

16

you? But about Jake, I'm betting he's already missing me. I can just see him now, wandering around the house sobbing for me. Wondering what it is he's going to have to do to get me back. Well, it's going to be different, that's for sure." She wasn't sure about the sobbing part, but she knew that he'd take her back in a heartbeat. The man wouldn't be where he was right now without her. "Jake will do just what I tell him to do. I know that he's had some rough times of late what with all those charge card bills that he had to pay off, but I'm sure by now that he's thinking what a mistake he made in cutting me off. I have him wrapped around my little finger."

Her mother huffed at her. Carol wondered why she'd come to see her when all she had to do was give Carol some money and her credit card. But she hadn't. Her mother was very untrusting too. Carol glared at her mother, wondering how on earth she'd had such a horrible person in her life all these years. Carol thought they'd all be better off if she would just die. Or be killed. That would be a better pay off in the insurance for her daddy.

"In the meantime, I'm paying for this room and the storage units you had to have to store all that crap in. Why on earth you had to take everything is beyond me. Or for that matter, why you'd want to. It's the ugliest shit I've ever seen. If I were Jake, I'd be pissed about you buying it in the first place. Were you trying to prove some point by going out and finding things that no human would possibly want in their garage, much less their home?" Carol waved her mom off. There was no accounting for some people's tastes, she thought. "Carol, he might not care a fig that you've left, have you thought of that? You said yourself that he's been cutting you off more and more all the time. Perhaps he's finally gotten sick of you spending all that money. You nearly ruined him once; perhaps he'll be thrilled to death that you've finally left and taken those things with you."

"Mother, you just don't understand our relationship. Once he sees the error of his ways, he'll be running back to me. You'll see. I'll call him on Monday and then you'll see that I'm right. He might even be calling me before then. Jake isn't all that smart, and he won't be able to fend for himself in that big empty house without me there to guide him." Actually, Carol was surprised that he'd not called her last night or this morning. Surely he'd seen what she'd done to him. At the very least, he would've seen the note she'd taken the time to leave him. "I had to take a stand in this. It's the only way that he's going to learn anything."

"He's not stupid, Carol. Jake is a smart man, and I think you're overestimating this hold you think you might have over him. As I said, he's more than likely dancing a jig around the room and buying things that he likes and not you." She asked her mother what she was talking about. "You think that you have him by the balls. I'm pretty sure, since he's cut you off so nicely, that he has taken them back and will use them. I don't think you realize what a bitch you've been to him."

"Mother, if you can't be nice to me in my time of need, then perhaps you should just go home. I'm settled now. But the next time I want you to bring me money and a credit card, just have one of the servants do it. Or Daddy." Her mom huffed again. "Why are you always treating me like I'm the bad guy? Jake just needs to learn that I'm the best thing that has ever happened to him. Once he does, then things will start to go back to the way I want them. No more cutting me off just because he said. I'm a grown woman, and have needs that he doesn't understand."

"Carol, I think he understands you more than even you do. As I've said time and time again, the man could have done much better than you." Her mother had always been so jealous of her, of her beauty, her husband. Even the way she decorated. "I'm going home. But as I told you when you called, I can only pay for you to stay here for two nights. I don't know why you have to have the best of everything. Had you gone cheaper, you could have had—"

"I do not do cheap. I'm an attorney's wife. I should have better." Her mom said something as she was moving out the door but Carol decided to ignore her. "If I need to stay more than you paid for, I'll let you know. I still don't know why you've put a limit on my trying to get my marriage to work."

Two nights away from her would be just what Jake needed to get his head on straight. The nerve of the man thinking he could just cut her off after everything she'd done for him. And the sooner he figured out that he needed her around, the better he'd be. Laying back on the bed, she thought of the things she was going to do once she was back to the house.

"I'm going to sell off every stick of furniture that was in there and start over. The house needs a fresh look anyway." She'd thought about just setting it on the side of the road when she'd left him, but was afraid that he'd just lug it back in after she was gone. He'd do that too, embarrass her like that. "Then I'm going to have the pool enlarged, and we're going to have a staff too."

19

She didn't swim, didn't even know how, but her parents didn't have a pool so she wanted one. And the staff would make her day so much better. Just being able to say that to someone... "I have to talk to the staff," or "The staff has been so much trouble lately." It excited her to no end to think of someone asking her about how many she had.

They'd had staff at first...well, someone to cook for them. There had been cleaning personnel as well. A woman and her daughter had come in twice a week to dust and run the vacuum. But after the first large purchase that she'd made to redo the living room, he'd cut even that off.

The cook; Carol couldn't even remember why they'd left, but Jake had gone on for over an hour about how she was to treat people that worked for them. Carol thought that staff, no matter what they did for her, needed to cater to her needs more than she did theirs. Thoughtless people. They needed to learn their place, and they would when she was back in charge.

The phone ringing startled her. As she picked it up, thinking it was her mother, she snapped at her to leave her alone. The silence at the other end made her pause. When she asked who was there, she was greeted with male laughter.

"I'm Forrest Stout. You must be Carol Lane Winslow." She said that she was just Carol Winslow. "For now. I'm calling on behalf of Jake Winslow. He would like to set up a meeting with you in the near future."

"You tell him when he cuts me off, I cut him off. And what do you mean, for now?" The man laughed again and she positively abhorred him. "Who are you anyway? One of his buddies from work? Never mind. You tell Jake that I will come home when he has his priorities right. If you'd like to take him my demands, I can read them off to you. There won't be any more cutting me off. I demand that—"

"No, I won't be taking him anything of the kind. But as for being his friend, I've never had the pleasure of meeting Jake, but I think, just because he left you, I could be his best friend. I have, however, spoken to his grandmother. Jenna and I go way back." Carol didn't care. She didn't care for the elderly Winslow any more than she did Jake's parents. "What time can you meet with us, Carol? I'd like to get this over with for him so that he can move on with his life."

"I'm not going to meet with him at all until I get some reassurance that what I want is taken care of. You tell him that." He said that he would. "Aren't you even going to ask me what I want? And I don't appreciate you cutting me off. I don't know who you think you're talking to but—"

"No, I'm reasonably sure neither of us want to know what you might want. And I'm also sure I've got you figured out. Oh, and while I have you on the phone, you should know that the locks have been changed on the house and the garage that you shared with Jake. Also, the things that you have in storage, they're being removed even as we speak and moved to the address that you put on the receipt. I'm sure your parents are going to just be thrilled. You have a nice day."

She was still standing there holding the dead receiver when she thought of what he'd said to her. Why would Jake change the locks? Was he afraid of someone robbing them? There wasn't shit in the house. That, to her, was locking the barn door after the horse got out. Or something like that. Her dad said that all the time, and she was happy to think that she knew that one. Also, what did he want a meeting for? Why not just have her come back to the house? She put the receiver in the cradle of the phone and sat on the bed. She wondered too what he'd said about the storage and how that would make her parents happy. Her mother wasn't getting her things.

"What are you up to, Jake?" She thought about calling him, asking him straight up what he was doing, but that would interfere with her plans. He was going to beg her to come home, and her calling him wasn't on her list. "You aren't playing by my rules, Jake, and that will only make this harder on you."

She went to the lovely desk that hadn't been in the room when she'd gotten there. A few well-placed calls, everyone understanding that she was a lawyer's wife, had not only gotten her the desk, but also free usage of the mini-bar.

The Jake list, as she'd begun to call it, was pretty good if she did say so herself. There were some things marked off on it already. And things were going along just the way she wanted them, also in the order that she wanted them. Carol was looking at number six that was as yet still unmarked. He should have called her by now. Again, he wasn't doing things the way she wanted them.

Number one had been having the house emptied. It had been difficult for her to find a mover that would do it all in one day. But her daddy had come through for her on that. He'd hired two firms to come in and take over. Of course she'd lied to Daddy, telling him that there were bugs in the house and that her lovely things were going to be ruined if they didn't get them out of the house, and he'd done it.

Her mother had shown up at her door while she was working on number two. Leave Jake a note.

"What are you up to, Carol? You can't have Jake's permission to do this to his home." She turned to her mom and glared. "You're going to regret this."

"No I'm not, I have a plan. And since this is my house, I don't need his permission, nor do I care if he has an opinion concerning my actions. This is all his fault anyway." She'd been thrilled to death to show her mother her list, and all she did was tell her she was ill-advised if she thought this was going to work. "Of course it'll work. I always get what I want."

"You've never gone this far before. I'm pretty sure that he's not going to do what you want this time, no matter how many lists you have and whatever order you put them in. It's bad enough that you've treated this man so poorly all these years, but to do this, to destroy his home.... Carol, I never thought I'd say this to my own child, but you're not right in the head."

Number three had been harder to get than she thought it would. Her mom didn't like to part with money any more than Jake did. But in the end Mother had put her up in a hotel. It was her plan to go live with her parents for a few days, but her mother had said no and had more than likely convinced Daddy that it was not a good idea. She was going to have a long talk with him once she was back in her home and with Jake. Mother was starting to get on her nerves, and she was sure her daddy would fix it.

Number four had been put in motion the moment she was set up in the hotel. Make sure that her friends knew where she was and why. Well, her version of why she was out of her home. She'd told them that she and Jake had had a terrible fight and she'd left him until he could cool down. That hadn't gone as well as she'd planned either, now that she thought about it.

Not a single one of her friends had been sympathetic to her. She'd expected them to rally around her, bad mouth Jake and his treatment of her, but not one of them had. Two had said they were too busy to talk and had hung up. Mercedes, the one that she'd thought the most of, who also had the most money of all her friends, had told her she'd be lucky if Jake didn't divorce her on the spot. And that she'd not blame him one single bit. The others hadn't taken any of her calls. Carol thought that since it was late in the year a lot of them had gone out of town. That had to be the reason.

Then there was number five. Five had been a spur of the moment add-on to her list. And possibly the worst thing she might have done. At least to the standpoint that it had gotten her the most grief. People weren't as receptive to her story as she'd hoped they'd be.

Going to the newspaper to tell them that Jake had hit her had been a huge undertaking. It had required her to pinch her mouth until it was puffy, and to wear dark glasses when it wasn't too terribly bright outside. Twice she'd walked into a wall, and once had tripped over the curb.

And for all that, she'd been humiliated once she'd entered the big building. Three of the people that had agreed to talk to her told her she was full of shit, and one of them had even told her she was lucky that he'd not hurt her worse. Carol tried to tell them that they didn't know Jake as she did, and was left in tears after they made fun of her.

Now here she was on number six, and she'd hit a wall. There had been no calls from Jake so that she could execute that part of her plan. She was going to tell him, no matter what he said, that she wasn't going to live like he'd wanted her to. She was going to tell him that she needed money to make her life better. That there had to be changes, too, in how they lived. Not only would there be a staff for her to order around, but she wanted a gardener as well as a limo driver. Each of her bullet points were left unchecked because her husband hadn't called.

"Damn it, Jake, what are you up to? And what is taking you so long to do what I need for you to do?" As she paced the room, she tried to think of reasons that he'd not called. His phone was dead? Not likely. He was the only person she knew that could go days on a single charge. He just never used his phone like normal people did. Did he forget her daddy's number? No, she'd made sure that it was programed into his phone the moment he'd gotten it. There wasn't any reason she could think of that he'd not have been able to call.

That man that had called, Stout, he alleged he'd talked to Jake. She knew that had to mean that his phone was still working and it was charged. They didn't own a house phone, again because Jake said it would be a waste of money, so that couldn't be it. Then she wondered if he was working late again.

Jake did work on Saturdays a great deal. She thought it had been because he was going to ask for an increase on the limits on his cards, but then he'd gone and canceled them all. But even working on Saturday didn't negate the fact that he should have called her. Nothing was as important as him calling and begging her to come home. His calling was the thing that was going to get her what she'd wanted. Carol decided that she was going to make him suffer more for this, and smiled as she added that to her list.

CHAPTER 2

Forrest closed the file he'd been occupied with for the last several hours and stretched. He'd been working on this case pretty hard and needed a break. What he really wanted to do was break the little scammer's neck, but he wasn't a violent man. Not usually anyway. As he stood up and went to his bathroom, he thought of the woman who he was now going to ruin. It wasn't a matter of if he was going to do it, but when and how. Jenna had told him to not hold back when it came to ending the marriage of her grandson.

Carol Winslow was a first class cunt. And for as much as he hated to use that word, he thought it fit her perfectly. She'd been ruling the roost for far too long, and now she was going to get her comeuppance. Or at least he hoped so. And he thought he might enjoy it more than he had any other case he'd ever been on. When his phone rang, he made his way back to his desk and answered it. Few had the private number that rang here, and he had an idea who it might be. Jenna had been checking up on him since he started on this divorce yesterday.

"You should know that she is, as of this moment, trying to get my grandson into trouble with the law. Something about spousal abuse." Forrest loved Jenna as much as he had his own mom when she'd been alive. "I'm telling you, Forrest, this woman has to go down for all the trouble that she's caused my grandson. She has to. I never liked her as a teenager, and absolutely loathe her as an adult."

"She will get what she deserves and more if I can help it. I promise." She huffed. "I'm sorry, did you say that you trusted me? Was that what I heard?"

"You know that I'd trust you with everything I have. And I have since I first approached you right out of college." He just laughed. "Forrest, you have to make sure that he comes out all right with this. You have no idea how long this has been going on. Jake needs to be able to move on from this. Get on with his own life for a change instead of catering to her every whim and cleaning up all her messes."

"He will, Jenna. I swear to you; I'm going to do my best for him. As for her messes, I'd say even before they were wed Carol was into one thing or another. I've been doing some research on your girl. I know that you're aware that she didn't pay property taxes for two years, and you had helped Jake out with that. But there were other situations that I don't think anyone was aware of. Lucky for Jake he was notified at work or he might have lost it all. One of the smartest things he could have done was put things in your name. But did you know what she did with the money?" She asked him if she'd been shopping again. "Yes,

28

that's what I would have thought too. No, she used the money for an abortion. Not once, but twice over the course of their marriage. There could have been more, ones that I can't track down, but she's been a very wayward girl. And so you know, I don't think either of the babies were Jake's. She was having numerous affairs throughout their marriage, mostly with men that Jake thought of as friends. Jake said that they slept in separate rooms for most of their lives together, so that leads me to believe that she didn't take their vows all that seriously from the beginning."

"Does Jake know?" Forrest told her that he did now. "Well, if this didn't close that door with her, I don't know what will. But I actually think that he's happy about this. When he came to my home for breakfast this morning, I could have sworn that he was excited for this next chapter of his life to get under way. He told me that he'd actually spent most of last night ordering things that he wanted for his home. This has been very liberating for him."

"When I spoke to him this afternoon to ask him when he would like to set up a meeting, he told me that he was furniture shopping. I told him that I could get his things back for him, but he said that he wanted fresh and his choices. I asked him what he wanted done with the things and he told me to send them to her parents, since he was sure that was where she was staying. She's not, but I sent them there anyway. They should arrive there in a couple of days. I had a blast making that wish come to fruition for him. That did not sound like a man that was on the bad end of a divorce." He laughed. "I cannot wait to meet him, Jenna. After all the things you told me about him, I'm sure

I'm going to like him a great deal."

"He'll adore you as much as I do. Especially now that he's getting things finished up with her. Tyler and Belinda did a horrible thing raising her up like they did. I'm telling you, Forrest, they should have beaten her more." He leaned back in his seat and thought of how much this woman knew about him and his own parents. And the debacle that had been what he thought was the love of his life. "I can almost hear your thoughts, young man. I will not have you being depressed about anything right now. You're going to be fine, just like my grandson is going to be."

"I really screwed up with Thomas, Jenna. I don't know what happened. Everything about him and us was a lie. And the fact that he stole from me, and I sort of let him, hurt me more than I think anyone can know." She told him that she understood and that she was sorry. "Thank you so much. But it's been five months. Do you suppose I'll ever trust anyone again?"

"Yes, I really do. And I think you're not so much upset about this as you are lonely. You need to meet you a nice man, show him your lovely cat, and live together happily ever after. You deserve that." He looked at his computer when it notified him of a message. He was sure that Jenna heard it and laughed when she spoke again. "I have to go myself. You go on and set up whatever you need to, and I'll make sure that my boy is there. And Forrest? You keep your chin up. This too will work out. You can bank on that."

After he hung up, he sat there for several minutes before he opened his inbox. There were several emails there, most of them from his own attorney, Paul. Thomas Simpson, his former lover—and thief—was suing him for breach of promise and a whole plethora of other things. And unlike Jake's suit, this wasn't going to be easy, but messy as fuck.

Thomas had been a bartender in a sleazy bar when he'd met him. The only reason Forrest had even gone into the place was because he'd been meeting a client. It wasn't his usual haunt. The place had had one redeeming thing, and that had been Thomas. Or so Forrest had thought.

Their relationship started out quickly. Too quickly, he knew that now. Forrest wasn't sure who had initially started it, or how they'd ended up back at his place. But within hours, just hours, not only was the man in his bed, but he'd moved a few of his things in as well. Forrest thought he should have seen the red flags even then. Then one morning, about three months after their first night, he noticed that some of his things were missing. Then his bank called.

He'd been on his way to work and was looking at his phone when the call came in. For some reason—and he did find out later that Thomas had done it—the calls were muted, and he would have missed the call from the bank had it not been for the fact that he'd been on his phone when the call came in. Answering on the third ring, he could tell that the bank manager, Roger Wayne, was in a tizzy.

"Your friend, Thomas, he's been in here several times over the last few days trying to add his name to your accounts. I just didn't know what to do without you here. And to be honest with you, Forrest, I was surprised by it. That just didn't sound like something you'd do. I mean, you're a generous man, but I don't think you'd be that lavish. Not with your own money."

He asked him if he'd added him yet. "No, no. I explained to him that it would take three business days. A lie, I'm sorry to say, but without talking to you, I thought it best in this incident. I was nearly ready to go by your home to see if he'd murdered you off or something. I'm so glad I got you today. I just thought that your signature just didn't look right. Close but no cigar, as my grannie used to say."

Forrest wanted to go back in the house and confront Thomas. To demand for him to tell him what else he'd been up to. But he had an idea that Thomas had played this hand before, and would have been very careful in his movements. Roger explained how he'd had all the right forms, knew just what signatures were needed and why.

"I'll be there in a few minutes. But can you do me a favor? I'd like for you to open another account for me, please. And when I get there, I'll transfer all my money to that one." Roger said he could do that as he laughed. "Then we'll add him to the account that he wants on. Plus, that will get him in big trouble if he's forged my name to paperwork."

On the way in, he made several more calls. The first was to a lock company to go out to his apartment with the landlord's permission and to change the locks. He wanted them changed as soon as Thomas left for the day. Then he had a cleaning crew set up to come in and clean his place from top to bottom, including sending his suits and all clothing out to be cleaned. Forrest wanted no traces of the man anywhere near him, and if it cost him a little to get it done, it was well worth it. Yes, it was rash and quick, he knew this, but in his heart, he knew it was the right thing to do. Cutting the tie quickly and sharply.

Roger had everything ready when he got to the bank. Not only was the forgery of his name pretty close, the account number and routing numbers were correct. One of the things missing from his home had been a check from his checkbook. Now he knew just where it had gone. The only thing Thomas didn't have, for which Forrest was happy, was his social security number. Thankfully, like most people, he didn't carry the card in his wallet any more.

By the time he made it to his office later that morning Forrest had called the police, and had made arrangements to have all the other things that he'd been missing reported and the security team at his offices on alert. Forrest was ready for the showdown. And it wasn't long in coming.

The phone call came in just after two in the afternoon. Forrest had been knee deep in a file when he simply reached over and answered. He smiled the moment he heard Thomas's voice on the other end of the phone.

"I've been arrested. Can you please come down here and help me out? I just don't know what's going on." Forrest told him he was really busy at the moment. "Forrest, they're putting me in a cell. I need for you to come down here and straighten things out. They won't even tell me what is going on. And I think that someone has messed with your locks. I can't get into our apartment either."

"Straighten what out, Thomas? The fact that you tried to clean out my account? Or is it the paintings and artwork that you've sold off that I should help you find? I'm confused as to why you'd think I'd help you out any more than I have already. As for you having access to my apartment and my things, I've taken care of that myself." Thomas started talking about gifts and how he'd given them to him. "No. I'm a nice guy to a point, but I'm not that nice. Nor am I stupid. One thing I've never given you was trust; also no gifts, no money, nor have I ever given you any kind of indication that you could get into my bank accounts. How far were you going to take this before you left? My car? My home? I'd really like to know what you thought you were doing."

"So this is how it's going to be, is it? Well I have news for you, Forrest. You and I, we were nothing." Forrest said he had that right. "You were just another notch in my bed. And you know what? You weren't that good of a lay either. Fuck you, Forrest. I'll win this in the end. I always do."

"Yes, you might have before me, but don't think this is going to just go away. I'm not one to fuck with. You should have figured that out a while ago." As he hung up the phone, he heard Thomas talking about the others, how he'd taken them, but Forrest had had enough. After laying the phone in the cradle, he sat there for several minutes before he realized he was no longer alone in his office.

"Bad news?" He nodded at Jenna. "Bad news, Forrest, or is it just something that came along at a bad time? You don't look like a man who has lost a lot, but hated that you've been taken. Is that what it is?"

"I'm not sure what you mean." She nodded. "This guy, I was living with him and he tried to rob me. Well, I guess he did. I don't think this is the first time either."

"Mostly he hurt you. And I doubt it's the first time, either, if he got by you. Thieves and dickheads seem to get away for a long while before they finally fall. You're going to make him fall, aren't you?" Forrest nodded, feeling the tears fill his eyes. "I would imagine that he's out there now crowing to the world about how he got to sleep with the great and powerful Forrest Stout." The burst of laughter had him smiling at her.

"Not so much, I'm afraid. More than likely he's going to be trying to get more out of me." She told him not to worry about things that had no worth. "I could be ruined by this."

"Could you? I don't think so. But then, I'm not a gay man on the cusp of finding his feet. What did you think—just curious— was going to happen when you took him to your home? I don't think you ever really trusted him, did you? I mean, you told me yourself that you'd not even bothered having his name put on your stationary."

"Jenna, you are a hard woman." She laughed when he did. "I don't know that I did, no. I was happy, I think."

"You can't *think* you're happy, young man. You are or you're not. Were you?" Forrest didn't even have to think about it, and shook his head no. "See there, you knew this was coming and you're a better man for it. There is someone out there for you. A mate, I think you call it. Now, young man, gird up your loins and take him to the cleaners, and be done with it. He'll regret tangling with you."

"I hope so. And there is no mate for me, Jenna. Gay tigers just don't find their mates." She asked him why not. "Because how do you think that would go over? Hey, I'm your mate for all time, but also I change into an enormous tiger and can eat you alive. I'd like to, as a matter of fact."

"Sexually, I'm assuming on the eating part." He felt his face heat up as he nodded. "I'm not like most older people, in the event you haven't realized that. I go with the flow of things. I read up on things I don't know, and ask questions when I think the person answering them has a head on his neck and not between his legs. When I first met you, I asked questions enough that I could do some research on your kind. Not a lot out there, sadly. Most of it bodice rippers about sex. But I did read, over and over, that there was one special person for everyone. You just have to wait for them. Are you going to wait, Forrest, or go willy nilly into the next relationship that might get you killed? So you know, I hope you wait. I'd very much like to see you happy."

"I'll wait if you wait with me. Or perhaps you and I could live together, and we could be our own little pride." She shook her head. "You don't think we'd make a perfect couple?"

"I think—and this could just be me—but I think you're full of shit." Forrest had laughed hard, harder than he had in a long while. "But as for living with me, should you like to do that, you'd have to be very careful of the men I bring in. I may be nearing eighty, but I still like a good romp in the bed on occasion."

Forrest thought of her every time he had a bad thought enter his head about this thing with Thomas. He thought of her and what she'd say whenever he was having some difficulty about a case or just life in general. She was a good balm for his otherwise bad day. As he looked over the emails, most of which he deleted, he wondered if Jenna's grandson would be anything like her. For some reason he doubted it. There could only be one Jenna Winslow.

~~~

Carol was sick of waiting on someone to help her, especially Jake. And she had to be out of the hotel in the morning. Who made a person vacate a room by eleven in the morning when there were more important things to do than that? She wanted all day to lounge around, soak in the huge tub, and be pampered while she plotted and planned what she was going to do when she got back to her home. But her mother had told her this was her last night, and not even talking to her dad had helped her extend her stay. He'd told her that she was costing them too much money.

"But Daddy, you have no idea how I've suffered. And why do you care how much this is costing? You have a lot of money." He asked her about the bugs, and it took her a moment to think of what he was talking about. "There were some."

"No there weren't, Carol. I had those men go there and check each piece out, and there was nothing there. You lied to me. And you know what I think of liars. After all I've done for you, this is how you treat me? No, I will not gainsay your mother on this. You're out by tomorrow first thing or they'll come to you for the rest." She asked him why he was taking her mom's side. "I'm taking the side of the right way this should have been done. Your mother and I talked it over, and we've decided that you've done this all on your own. Jake might not be the best husband for you, but he's what you wanted and I made sure you had him. At a great cost to myself. Work this out, or so help me, Carol, I will be done with you."

Hanging up on him had been hard as her daddy meant the world to her. Everyone was against her. And damn it, Jake wasn't playing right either. He should have been devastated by now and begging her to return home. But she'd not heard a word from him, only that attorney who kept calling and asking for an appointment. She thought of what she'd seen last night when she'd taken a cab by her house.

There had been a big moving van out front, and the things they were unloading didn't look a thing like anything she would approve of. And she was pretty sure that Jake knew that too. Why, just the couch alone was as ugly as sin. Not a bit of style; just a dreadful brown color that made her think of poop.

She asked the driver what was going on. "Lady, in the event you don't know this, I'm a cabbie, not a clairvoyant. Why don't you get on over there and ask them? I just conveyed your butt here. I'm not doing any kind of prophesying for you."

Carol didn't care for the way he spoke to her and told him that. The man laughed and told her tough shit, then he took her back to her hotel at breakneck speed and told her to get out. She thought about not paying him—he'd treated her with no respect—but he put out his big beefy hand and told her that if she didn't pay in money, he'd take it from her in other ways. Carol had had to fork over the last of her cash she'd managed to take from her mother's purse when she'd not been looking.

Picking up the phone for the tenth time in as many minutes, she tried to think what she'd say to Jake when he answered. Crying hard was going to have to be the first thing he heard. Then telling him that she felt so abused by him. She was going to sob at just the right time when she explained to him how she hated the way he was treating her by taking her money. Also, she was going to have to mention that furniture. That was going to have to go. Pulling her notes to her, she went over each point as she pressed the buttons to put the call through. She was going to have to tell Jake that her phone was no longer working as well. The cell service, she'd been informed, had been cut off.

"Winslow residence." Carol thought she might have dialed the wrong number, because she had no idea who the voice belonged to except for the last name being said. "Winslow residence. May I help you?"

"I was looking for Jake. Jake Winslow, my husband. Who is this?" She was told that he was the new butler. "We don't have a butler. Are you there robbing the place? I'll call the police right now."

"I don't believe that a robber would answer the phone, do you? Nor do I think I'd get very far in my work if I did. Now, you say that you're the wife? Mr. Winslow has assured me that he is the only one that lives here. He had a wife, I suppose, but she left him for something better." She told the man that she'd left, but only temporarily. "I see. Well, actually I don't. But if you'd like to leave a message for Mr. Winslow, I can do that for you. I don't expect him home until later today."

"I need to speak to him now. Tell him that I'm coming over there so that we can talk." He told her again that Jake wasn't home. "Of course he is. It's Sunday. Even he takes that day off. Tell him that I want him to sit down and listen to what I have to say to him so we can get this cleared up."

"It's Tuesday." She wasn't sure he was right, but assumed, for now, that he was. "Mr. Winslow will be returning at five-thirty this evening. If you would like, I can give him a message. But I'm not telling him all that other stuff. Just that you called and your number. Is there one that I can give him?"

Carol wanted to scream. Jake wasn't doing anything in the order she wanted, not a single thing. After giving the number to the butler, she asked him to repeat it back to her twice so she knew he had it right. After hanging up, she thought about calling back just to ask his name, but decided he wouldn't be there long enough after she returned to learn it. Things were going to take a nice change when she got back to her home, and then Jake was going to explain a lot of things to her. Like how come he had a butler there now when she'd been begging for one for years.

Next, she called the furniture store whose name had been imprinted across the back of the truck delivering the furniture when she'd been there. She wanted answers and they were going to give them to her. Like what the hell were they doing delivering furniture to her home without her approval? And she wanted to know how many other things had been brought in. Was there anything with color on it? She needed to know just how much she was going to have to work to get things back to the way she wanted them. Jake was going to pay for doing this while she was out.

The phone was answered just as she was writing down some more things to talk to Jake about. "Yes, hello. I'd like to speak to your manager. There has been a dreadful mistake and I want it taken care of today." She was put on hold as she thought of what she was going to do first when she got home. After tossing out the other things, she was going to go on a shopping spree like none other. She might even go all the way to New York this time. When the line was opened, she told him who she was and why she was calling him. Before she could get into what she needed for him to do, he spoke.

"Mr. Winslow placed the order and had us deliver it to his home yesterday. I do believe he was quite happy with his things." She told him that wouldn't do. "I'm sorry. I don't understand. What won't do?"

"That monstrosity that you took there. I want you to go back and get it. It's not at all my taste. I would have thought that a person who owns a furniture store wouldn't sell such things, unless you cater mostly to the homeless. Is that it? No matter. You'll have to go out there and pick those things back up and take them away. I'll be out sometime over the next day or two to replace them. But only if you get there today. I cannot stand the thought that you've ruined my home with that monstrosity." Carol had heard that word used a couple of days ago and was glad that she was able to use it twice now in the same sentence. *Monstrosity*. It has a nice ring to it, she thought. As she waited for the groveling, the apologies that were due her, she decided to get her nails done as well. "Did you hear me? I said that you have to take care to make this right. Today. I am most upset, and you know as well as I that the customer is always right."

"In most cases, I would say that's correct, but not this one. It is my understanding, Ms. Lane, that you are no longer able to purchase for the Winslow household as you are not a resident there any longer. We were told that several times, not only by Mr. Winslow himself, but by his attorney." She opened her mouth to tell him that she would be taking care of that as well, but he continued before she could. "Mr. Winslow called here just an hour ago, telling me what excellent choices he'd made in his purchases. He said that it was not only the most comfortable thing he'd ever sat in since living in his home, but also that he wanted to get the rest of the set. Two chairs, as well as end tables and coffee tables. He is a man of good taste. So my advice to you is that, if you're going to be throwing around your weight, you should really check the facts first and foremost."

"I'm his wife." He didn't say anything and she had to think about how to salvage this. She needed this man to understand, but she had questions of her own. "You called me Ms. Lane. Why did you say that? I'm his wife. I'm still a Winslow until I say differently. And you can't talk to me this way. I'll have Jake own you for how you're treating me. He'll be really pissed off."

"As you wish, Ms. Lane." Carol wanted to scream at him to call her by her married name, but she hung up on him instead.

Jake wasn't playing by any of her rules, and worse yet, she had no idea how to make him understand that he needed to. She knew that he was missing her, he had to be. And she knew that he was doing this because he was lonely or depressed. That was it, her mind told her; he was depressed and lashing out the only way he knew how. Carol was going to have him eating out of her hand soon, and she couldn't have been happier about it. She was going to be able to get whatever she wanted from him because of this thing he was going through right now.

Going to the door when someone knocked, she was too happy and excited to check to see who it might have been. More than likely Jake, she told herself. She opened the door and stared at the man standing before her for a full minute before she realized he was speaking. Christ, he looked good enough

42

to eat and fuck.

"Are you Carol Lane Winslow?" She nodded. "Good. I thought I had the wrong room again. Here you go."

The thick envelope was shoved at her before she could figure out who he was. And when he put a pen in her hand and told her to sign on line ten, she did that as well. He smiled at her as he said she'd been served and just walked away. Carol wasn't sure what to think when he started laughing all the way to the elevator. People were very strange, she thought.

Taking the big blue envelope to her bed, she opened it up. Carol read the first line of it four times before she understood what she had been handed. Divorce papers? Jake was suing her for a divorce? She read it once more, and just to be sure, she read it aloud.

"In the marriage of Jake Anderson Winslow, ten-twenty Lawrence Park, Zanesville, Ohio," then it listed his social security number. "Petitioner. What the fuck is a petitioner?"

Carol wrote it down to ask her daddy when she spoke to him again, and continued to read until she got to the bottom where it said the word "respondent." Getting a headache from trying to figure this out, she decided to get some information from someone who always did what she wanted when she wanted. Picking up the hotel phone, she called her parents. Daddy answered on the first ring.

She told him what she had in her hand and asked him what it meant. Carol was really pissed and might have hung up on him when he started cursing, but she wanted answers. And since she had no one to ask but him, she had to endure his ill temper.

"He's gone and done it. The boy is going to have to cancel this shit right now. Yes, sir. He's going to cost me a pretty penny, but he's going to stop this nonsense today. As for what that says, he's divorcing you, Carol. He's gone out and grown some balls after all. And petition is the term for what you have in your hand. A formal document stating that he's gotten stupider in his years since you brought him home, a hell of a lot more irresponsible too if he thinks I'm going to just let this go." Carol asked him what respondent meant, even though she had a pretty good idea what it was now. "That would be you, the defendant in this. He's named you as the party that he's filed against. Holy damn, this is going to cost us both. Never thought he'd have the balls to do it. You had him so pussy whipped I thought for sure that he'd die an unhappy man. I just knew that you taking off the way you did was going to come back and bite me in the ass. And it has, my wallet too."

"Daddy, I don't care what he does to your wallet. He's divorcing me and you think this affects you somehow? That's not fair. He can't do this to me. He's even moving furniture into my home. I never gave him permission to do that." Her dad stopped swearing again and she thought she might have finally gotten through to him. "Daddy, you have to help me by talking to him. He can't do this. It's not in my plan."

"Your planning is going to put me in the poor house, Carol. I can't have you doing this to me again. Do you hear me? Not again. You've done nothing, not one thing, since the day you set your sights on him to give him an inch without it costing me a bunch of money. The things I've had to do for you…well, it just makes me sick. You cannot imagine the amount of money that

44

went to his father for you to have him. But this? It'll be nothing compared to what he's going to demand now. And how have you repaid me? Nothing. Not a damned thing. You have been sucking us dry, that's what you've done. All of us. When this gets back to his parents, there will be hell to pay. And I'm not sure I'm going to help you out with it either." He let out a long breath and she felt her heart twist up. Jake was turning her daddy against her. "I'm not going to help you, Carol. I'm going to have more going out than I can possibly afford right now."

Carol put the phone back and sat there on the side of the bed and cried. Her own daddy wasn't playing by her rules either. He'd been the one person in the world she could count on. And now he was treating her as badly as Jake was. She was going to have to do something soon, because she was going to be out of this hotel in a few hours and she had nowhere to go just yet. She glanced at her notes and decided she needed a new list. And she had to talk to Jake. He needed to get with the program.

CHAPTER 3

Jake wasn't sure how to conduct himself in another attorney's office. He'd been on the other end of the desk when dealing with people for a long time, but this was the first time that he could remember when he wasn't in charge. He decided that this side wasn't as nice as he'd thought it would be. When his grandma shifted on her seat, he looked over at her.

"You'll like Forrest. He's a good man and a better attorney. Did you know that he delivered the paperwork to Carol himself? Just so he could see her face? I wish I could have been there. I bet she was fit to be tied." Jake said he'd told him when he spoke to him yesterday. "Good. I guess she made a call to her daddy too. He called me right after to ask me for a meeting. I think that there is something there too, but I told him to speak to my attorney. Carol isn't right in the head; you've figured that out, haven't you?"

"Yes. She called the house yesterday too. Demanded to

speak to me about something. I told Harley to hang up on her if she calls back." Grandma told him good for him, but he should get his number changed. "I will. I thought her dad would be pissed off, but I had no idea that he'd call you. What do you suppose he wants from you? Oh yeah, then Carol called the furniture store where I bought some of my things. I'm really glad you told me to make sure that everyone knew she wasn't on my charge cards anymore. I think you might have saved me a great deal of money."

"From what I've been able to find out, I think there was more to you marrying his daughter than was told. And I think perhaps your father knows a little about it as well. I also believe that at one point, he told her you were a good man and that you deserved better. But Carol usually gets her way." Jake nodded. He was coming to figure that out as well. "I heard you got a few things delivered yesterday."

"Oh yes. It's great. I even called to get the rest of the set. The couch is as soft as butter and smells so good. I took a nap on it last night and swear I've never slept better. My bedroom set is coming tomorrow. And I've decided to hire Harley to come in and cook for me full time. It's really nice to have someone there when I come home, and a hot meal as well. He's is wonderful; thank you for telling me about him. I think I've turned over a new leaf."

"It shows." Jake grinned. "I've not seen you this happy in a long time, Jake. I'm so glad that you're finally doing something for you."

"I'm not saying that it's been all roses and wine. I mean, for all the things that I find that make me feel good about myself and doing this, I find out more and more about Carol and her misdeeds. Forrest told me that Carol has had two abortions since we were married. And one of those in the last year. We don't even reside on the same floor of the house, much less sleep together. It's been a couple of years now since I've touched her. How did she think she was going to get away with this, Grandma?" He didn't feel as embarrassed as he thought he should talking to her about this. Grandma was his rock. "I guess I've been a fool."

"Not a fool. But a man that has been dealt a shitty hand. This will get better. See if it doesn't." He nodded and leaned back in his chair. "Jake, don't let her talk you into letting her back in your life."

"No. I won't. She's gone as far as I'm concerned. I can't do her way of living again. I guess I realized how bad it was with her, but not how it was making me feel all the time. I was hurting, and I don't mind telling you that I think she was making me sick as well. The stress of trying to guess what she was up to was taking its toll on me." Jake looked at his grandma. "You were right about her all along, it appears. But I did have a learning experience. Not a nice one, but I did learn."

When the door opened behind him he stood and looked at the man there. Christ, Jake thought, he was huge. But the longer the man stood there just staring at him, Jake began to feel uncomfortable. Well, that wasn't all of it; he was feeling something odd as well.

"Forrest?" The man turned to look at his grandma when she spoke. "What is it? Are you unwell? Has Carol said or done something to harm you?"

49

"No. I've not seen her since…. Is this a joke?" Jake looked at his grandma to see what the man was talking about. He wasn't sure even after glancing in her direction. "This can't be right, Jenna. What have you done? Are you trying to make me feel better or something?"

"I don't know what you mean. This is my grandson, Jake Winslow. Jake this is — " His grandma stood up then, her entire body stiff. And when she started laughing, Jake was more confused than before. "Oh Forrest. You've found him, haven't you? This is wonderful. I'm so happy for you."

"Well I'm certainly not. You don't understand, Jenna. This can't happen to me." Forrest moved into the room but walked as far from Jake as he could go, even pressing against the wall as he went. When he was seated in his chair, the man looked broken. "I don't know what's going on right now. This can't be real…it's surreal is what it is."

"What are you talking about? Maybe if I understood, I could help you." Forrest started to laugh, then looked at him. It wasn't a humorous laugh; more of a saddened one. Like he was too upset to cry and laughing was all he had. "I'm sorry. I don't understand."

"You won't after I tell you either. Or I don't think you will. Not yet at any rate." Jake sat back down but he wasn't sure if he should stay or go. The man was upset about something, and he had a feeling that it was bad. "If you don't mind, I'd just like to get this part with your divorce finished up. Then we'll…I guess we can talk then if you'd like. Okay, so I talked to your soon to be ex-wife yesterday. She called here just as I was leaving. She told me to tell you that you're not allowed to divorce her."

"That sounds like something she'd say. She was forever telling me what I could and couldn't do. I think that's why I... are you sure you're all right? We can do this some other time if you wish." Jake wanted to...well, he wanted to hold the man. Tell him that things would be better. Whatever they were. And he didn't understand that any more than he did what was going on. "Perhaps you should just tell us and then you'll feel better."

"I just don't know if this.... You know what a shifter is?" Jake told Forrest that he knew several. "I would have thought so. And I'm assuming that you have no opinion about them either way."

"If you mean that it doesn't bother me what they are, then yes, you'd be correct. I don't care what a person is, just how they treat those around them. Did Carol say something about one of them? She cannot stand the thought of...well, anything that is not what she wants." Jake laughed slightly. "She's a horrible person. I mean, I guess I knew that all along, but things are beginning to take shape in my head now. I'm very sorry if she insulted one of your friends. She is, as you said, not a nice person."

"It wasn't me or anyone that I know, but I thank you for that. I'm a cat, Jake. A tiger, as a matter of fact. Born one, even though my father is a human." Jake nodded, not sure what he was supposed to say to that. "Do you know much about shifters? Other than what you read? What I mean is, have you talked with one of my kind? About anything?"

"Not much. A little. I know that they can shift when they need or when their other part thinks they need to. They mate for life and it's usually a good relationship. Not all, but most of them are good. I've never taken a domestic violence nor a divorce case for any of them, so that's all I have to go on." Jake smiled at him. "I think there is more, but right now I'm more concerned with what is going on with you. Is there anything at all that I can do for you?"

"Let me tell you this first, then we'll see what you want to do. Yes, we mate for life. And we don't abuse or divorce for that very reason. I know there are bad relationships between mates...my father hated my mother and me too because of what we were. But for the most part, it's a long and very loving relationship. Christ, this is harder than I thought it would be." Jake waited for him to continue. "I'm homosexual. A gay shifter male that was without a mate until today."

"Okay." Jake glanced at his grandma then back at Forrest. "Perhaps you should just say whatever it is."

"You're my mate, Jake." Whatever Jake had thought he was going to say, that would never have entered his mind. "I would like to know what you're thinking right now, please."

"To be honest, I don't know. My mind is blank." Forrest nodded. "I was married. To a woman. And she wasn't...I wouldn't have picked her, I don't think. I shouldn't have married her at all, but I was sort of pressured into it. Why, I have no idea, but.... I'm babbling, I'm sorry. But for me to be your mate, your male mate, I'm not...I don't know what to think."

"Yes, I'm aware that you've been married to a woman." Jake's mind suddenly filled with questions. And images. Then he was afraid. "I want to touch you. No, that's not right, I need to touch you. But I won't."

"Why?" Jake felt his face heat. "I mean, why would you say that? Does it matter that you won't touch me?"

"I don't want to just touch you, Jake. I want a great deal more." His body warmed, then heated. Jake was confused not just by his feelings, but the thoughts that were racing in his mind. "Maybe we should just get through this, like I said, then if you want to talk, we can."

"Yes. All right." When he was handed a file, he stared at it for several seconds before he spoke again. "I don't know what to do. This is not anything that I've ever thought of in a long.... This is...I don't mean to sound crass, but I'm just unsure of everything about this."

"I understand. If you'd like, I can recommend someone else to take over your case. I know —" Jake told him no. "All right then. Let's begin. As you can see from the folder you have, Carol had asked her parents to help her leave you. But under false pretenses. The furniture was removed because she told her father that there was a bug infestation in the house, and it was important that things were removed before the exterminators arrived. I've spoken to them both, and believe it or not, they're willing to testify that she left you and the house you shared. Mr. Lane, I'm not sure what he has going on at the moment, but he sounds sort of resigned to the fact that this is beyond his control. And Mrs. Lane has told me that she wants this finished. Now."

"Is that important? That they testify, I mean?" Forrest explained. "But I don't care that she's gone from the house. I'm glad that she's absent. Nor that she took all the furniture. It was repugnant anyway." Forrest and his grandma laughed

53

and Jake joined them. It was the first good laugh he'd had in a while. "I want this to happen; I want her out of my life for good. Whatever it takes, I'd very much like her not to be a part of my life from now on."

"We'll get you there. But as for them testifying, it goes to show that she didn't want the house or she would have stayed and asked you to leave. Maybe she did, but by her own actions, she left you the house. And I'm hoping the courts will see it that way as well." He told him how the house was in his grandma's name. "Did Carol know this? I mean, was she aware that it was done and why?" Jake looked at his grandma when she laughed a little.

"Oh yes, she knows. And was not too happy about it either, let me tell you. I lent them the money for back taxes when she hadn't been paying them. They were close to losing it all due to foreclosure. Carol, along with Jake, signed the deed over to me. Jake insisted on it once I paid it off for them. When he asked me for a loan, we agreed that the house was supposed to be in my name only until he paid me back, but it didn't change." Grandma looked at him. "I never brought it up to be switched back because I was afraid that Carol would do it again. With my name on the deed, then the bank would call me if there was a problem. I never meant for you to pay me back, Jake. I was glad I could help you."

"He was smart to do that, Jenna. Both in paying you back and giving you the house as collateral. And the fact that she was well aware of it is perfect. She can't claim that the house belongs to her. Who brokered the deal?" Jake told him the bank. "Good. That's good. The bank will have had a vested interest in keeping things on the up and up."

Jake watched Forrest make notes, using his computer to look up phone numbers when he didn't know them. Jake did the same thing when he worked, not relying on someone else to gather information for him. He thought he'd like to work with him, be a partner in a law firm together. Jake didn't know why; he'd just met the man, but he thought he'd be a good person to work with. Jake looked at his grandma when she poked him.

"Your phone is ringing." Apologizing, he pulled out his phone and said it was Carol's dad. Forrest asked him to answer it, and if he wouldn't mind, put it on speaker phone. He nodded and did as requested.

"Jake?" It was Carol, not her dad. Forrest showed him a recording device. Jake nodded for him to turn it on. "Jake, I know that you're there. I can hear you breathing. What the hell have you done to me?"

"To you? I'm not sure what you mean, Carol. You're the one that left me, remember?" Forrest put a sheet of paper up, telling him to inform Carol that he was recording their conversation. "Carol, I want you to know that I'm recording this. I don't want you to—"

"You think I give a shit what you record, Jake? I don't. What I do care about is what you're doing to my house. And what do you mean by sending me this paperwork thinking that you want a divorce? You don't. I want you to make sure that whoever you've talked to knows that as well. You aren't getting a divorce from me. Not unless I say so. I like things just the way they were before you got all this in your head. I was teaching you a lesson. One, I might add, that you've not gotten.

55

You're not being very nice to me, Jake. And I don't care for it."
He started to explain to her how she'd left him no choice. "I
left you plenty of choices. Like not to cut off my credit cards
like you did. Not to take away my spending power. How am
I supposed to be with my friends if you're forever making me
look bad? Giving me what I wanted when I wanted it was what
you should have been doing. Not this…this divorce thing. I
won't stand for it, Jake. Make them stop this nonsense right
now."

"I'm not going to stop it. I like things the way they are
now. Carol, we couldn't afford you doing those things you
were doing. I don't have that kind of money to be tossing away
whenever you wish. You've nearly bankrupted us as it is. And
you left me, I didn't leave you." She made a noise, something
like the sound of a raspberry on a child's belly. "What was I
supposed to think when you emptied the house of everything
and even cut up my suits?"

"I did that to get you to see I mean business. You seemed
to have forgotten that I'm the one that has to stay at home all
day while you work to make money. What are you going to
do now? And just so you know, I'm not going to allow you to
leave that furniture in my home once I'm back there either." He
asked her what sort of business she meant to teach him. "That
you cannot take things from me when I want them. Jake, why
are you buying new things for the house? You know as well
as I do that those things are not my taste. There is no color on
them. Nothing to say power. I have that, Jake, all the power in
the world, and I will not have you taking it from me."

"I never bought it with you in mind." He heard her sharp

intake of breath and felt empowered by it. "As for your power over me? That's gone as well. I've enjoyed you being gone, as a matter of fact. It's been enlightening. And freeing. I've never slept better or felt so wonderful in my entire life. No, I think I like things just the way they're headed. The divorce is going ahead. I'm glad I'm getting it done."

"No, you're not, Jake. I want you to listen to me and stop this drivel right now." He asked her what drivel that would be. "You thinking that you know what it is you want or need. You know you don't want this. You're just acting out. Or you're depressed that I'm not there. That's all. I'll come home and bring my things back, and you'll see. It'll be just like it was before. You'll give me back my credit cards and I won't have to do this to you again." The second note went up and he nodded.

"Can you tell me about the abortions, Carol?" The silence on the other end was laughable to him. "There were two that I know of. The more I find out about you the more I think you've never been faithful to me, nor did you have any intentions of being so. I know that at least the last one wasn't mine. Who was it? Did you know him?"

"Who told you? James? Did he call you? I told him you'd not care. But now that it's out, yes, I had three as a matter of fact. None of them were yours. What does it matter? I'm willing to forgive you." He asked her what he had to be forgiven for. "You treated me badly, Jake. You know that. When I asked you for things, you said no. What sort of person does that to the person he's supposed to love? Where did you find out these terrible things, anyway? Was it James or Tayler? I'm telling you right now, they're not going to be getting into my bed after this.

But that's water under the bridge. You're going to give me what I want, aren't you, Jake?"

"No. I think I've given you enough. I've filed for divorce and I'm going to leave it the way things are. The fact that you have no shame in what you've done and just expect me to act like it never happened shows just what sort of person you are." He felt like a failure in that moment. Not for not loving his wife…because in that moment, he knew that he never had. But he'd let the woman he married take everything from him. "Carol, I don't know what your plans are, but I would suggest you get yourself a good attorney. Or a bad one, I don't care. But I am proceeding with this. I've had enough."

"Damn it, Jake, what is wrong with you? You will not treat me this way, do you hear me? I want you to get that crap out of my house and pay for my things to be brought back home, my home. Now, this is what you're going to do; I'll meet you there in the morning. After you've had time to think of what you've done to me and put my house back the way I had it. There wasn't any reason whatsoever for you to go out and try to shame me by putting that tasteless couch in there." He told her that he'd changed the locks. "Jake, you're starting to piss me off. I'm not going to take this from you."

"Good. I'm glad that you are pissed. And I'm not going to take you back. I'm not going to get rid of the things that I bought. Nor am I going to do a damned thing for you again." He laughed, feeling lighter for it; his failure, he only just realized, was not on him but her. "Goodbye, Carol. I'll see you in court."

When he closed the connection, he sat there for several minutes. He heard them talking, his grandma and Forrest. But what they said, he had no idea. Jake was getting a divorce. He was actually going to leave his wife by the curb. When he stood up, Forrest did as well.

"I need a drink." Forrest nodded and smiled. "I don't know what this thing is that you have going on, this other part of you, but if you'd come have a drink with me, I'd appreciate it. You and Grandma both."

~~~

Forrest watched Jake. He was calm, much too calm for a man who had just had his entire life turned upside down. Or maybe this was just him, the way he was. Calm and thoughtful before speaking. Forrest asked him twice if he was all right before he finally looked at him.

"My wife had affairs. Aborted children as if they were nothing more than an inconvenience to her. Spent money, the money I worked hard to earn, as if there was a limitless supply of it and no penalties if something else was set aside, just so that she could have things the way she wanted them." Forrest nodded. "But you want to know something really strange? I'm so relieved that I can hardly contain myself. Not about the abortions or the money, but that she's out of my life."

"I can understand that. The few minutes that you spoke to her on the phone, all I could think about was how you'd put up with her for ten years. And that I think she's a manipulative person who is finally getting her retribution." Jake nodded. "Are you all right, Jake?"

"Yes, I think I am. I mean, I have my moments, but all in all, I feel pretty good. Tell me about this mate thing." Forrest wasn't sure that now was the time and said as much. He was glad now that Jenna had begged off, saying she'd had enough for one day, and had left them to their own dinner and drinks. "What I mean is, I need something to distract me and I think that'll do it. Tell me. I need…I think I need to know."

"Jake, you don't have to do this. I'm sure we can find other things to talk about." Jake nodded but said nothing. "I'm thinking that the divorce will go off without a hitch. Once we file—"

"How does that work? Sex, I mean." Forrest shifted on his seat; this wasn't what he wanted to do. Not now. The man was very overawed right now. "You think that I'm off my rocker, don't you? That I'm only asking you these things because of Carol. I guess in a way I am, but you brought this up and I'd very much like to understand why you think I'm your other half. That's what it's called, right? Your other half?"

"Yes. And I don't think you're off your rocker. What I think is that you're overwhelmed. You're also stressed out and not thinking right. This is not something that I can take lightly with you. We have to.... This isn't something that you can just step into without thought." He asked him if it was because he was human. "That's part of it. The other part is that—and it's a big part—you're not a homosexual."

"How do you know? I don't." He asked him what he meant. "I mean, some of the things that are going through my head aren't anything that I've ever thought of before. But you want to know something? I'm not sickened by it. Nor am I afraid of you."

"But you might be." Jake shook his head. "I want you to think about this. About how you think it will feel if I take you home and to my bed."

"All right." Forrest wanted to scream. He wasn't making this easy for him. "Look, you think that I'm only doing this because...well, I'm not really sure what you're thinking. But I have been doing a lot of thinking. About a lot of things. One of them is the fact that I seem to be drawn to you. I'm not turned on; I don't think. But I feel...I feel something for you. Do you understand?"

"Yes, I do. And I'm drawn to you as well. But you can't just do this on a whim, Jake. If I take you to my bed, you will belong to me. None other but me. And if you decide that this is something you can't handle, it'll be too late for me." He asked him what that meant. "You're my mate. My other half. And if I commit to you, I can never go back. I'll die if I can't have you. I'll go rogue, and in that I mean I'll go insane. More so than I think I'm feeling right now."

"That's being really dramatic, don't you think?" Forrest said nothing. "You're serious. You'll literally die if I don't stay with you after one night?"

"Yes. I will either be killed by the pride leader because I can no longer handle me or my cat, or—and this is what normally happens—I will end my life. Because once you and I are together, life for me will never be the same. We either do this all the way or nothing. There is no in-between for me. You? Yes, but not for me." Forrest could see his struggle. Hell, he had his own struggles right now. The man was perfect for him. "Look. Let's just get through this divorce and you can figure things out."

"Is there a book?" Forrest told him sadly there was not.

"So other men, they've gone through this before, I'm assuming. What do they do for answers?"

"Jake, I'm trying to tell you, I don't think there are a lot of gay shifters out there. Especially with a human counterpart." Jake said nothing, just sat there staring into his beer. "Like I said, we should just get you divorced. Carol is not going to go away nicely; I think you know that. This other? Nothing may come of this, and then you and I can go our separate ways."

"Does it work like that?" Forrest told him he didn't know. "I have a lot to think about. I don't know a great deal about any of this, including what I'm going to do in the long term about my life. Not just anything that might happen between us — and I'm not saying it will — but with Carol, her parents.... Everything."

"I understand." He did too. It was a great deal to throw at someone. "I'm starved. How about we get some pizza or wings and then call it a night after we eat? It's been a rollercoaster day for both of us."

After they left the bar, going their separate ways, Forrest went to the edge of the property near his home and let his cat take him. He hadn't been out much lately, not since Thomas, and it felt really good to be free. Well, as free as a big tiger in a small town could be. As he roamed the woods, doing nothing more than chasing scents, he paused by the large lake at the back of his property.

Forrest thought about Jake. Not just him, he supposed, but what having him as a mate would be like. They'd be happy, of this he had no doubt. But they'd have trouble too. Not between the two of them, but with the world in general. He knew personally what a gay man in this world had to deal with, and not a lot of it was pretty or easy. And being a shifter on top of that just compounded those troubles tenfold.

The noise behind him had him lying low on the ground. He sniffed the air around him, even lifted his head up a little to see if he could locate the noise. There wasn't anything that he could see or smell, but he was still very cautious. As he lay there, his heart pounding in his chest, he thought of Jake and that maybe he'd come to see him. But the laughter, the soft laughter, had his heart skipping several beats. Then nothing.

CHAPTER 4

Carol paced her room. Living with her parents was certainly different now that she'd had a taste of freedom, but not in a good way. They were driving her nuts, especially her daddy. He was supposed to be on her side, and yet he kept saying she was lucky that they'd let her come back after all the things they'd heard about her. Carol didn't understand what their problem with her was, not really. It wasn't as if she'd filed for divorce.

"Well, that shit is not going to happen. I will not allow him to toss me away like I don't mean anything to him. I'm his world, and the sooner he figures that out, the better off he'll be." As she looked around the room, hating it, she realized how far she'd come since she grew up in this house, and that she'd not had the fashion sense then that she had now. "What was I thinking?"

Posters, old and out of date, hung on every wall. One even

had an ugly dog on it that had big sad eyes. She walked to it and tried to remember why she'd hang such a thing. And why on earth her mother would have let it still be there. Tearing it down, she felt satisfied and started tearing down the rest of the crap that she had at one time deemed perfect. Carol decided it was time to update some other things around here too.

It took her nearly an hour to get all the things off the wall. Then she grabbed up the trash can and started swiping things from the dressers and bathroom vanity into it. By the time she'd done all that she could with what she had to work with, the room was a mess and so was she. But she could almost see what she was going to do to this room and perhaps the rest of the house. Her daddy would be pleased with her again, and she'd be able to get him to help her with Jake. As he had before.

Going to the bathroom again, she turned on the water and stripped down. Carol looked at her body in the large mirror. Changes might be in store for her as well. Money was meant to be spent, she thought, and why not on her?

It wasn't perfect. It might have been had Jake just let her get the rest of her surgeries to make herself just the way that she'd wanted to be. Bigger breasts, pouty lips. She even wanted to get her thighs shaped up and toned looking. Her nose was the only thing she'd been able to get done, and that had been nearly five years ago.

She wasn't sure she'd ever be able to forgive him for taking all her money from the accounts and credit cards. But she supposed it was much better than living in a smaller house had they lost the big one. Who knew that paying your taxes on time was such a big deal? She looked at her belly.

Carol was glad now that she'd found out about the pregnancy when she had. She'd had to sell off some of her prettier things to get it taken care of, but it had been worth it. To be fat with a bastard would have been hard to hide when Jake took her back. And he would…soon too.

It hadn't been her fault that she'd gotten pregnant this last time, but she'd been the one that had been caught. The guy — she could no longer remember his name — had told her that he'd been fixed. Sure he was.

As she got into the shower to clean up, she wondered how Jake had found out about the other brats. Surely they had some sort of law that prohibited them from telling on her. Of course she'd not gone to a real doctor; she knew they kept records. But still, with him knowing that little bit about her, she wondered what else he might have been able to unearth. Dressing in the bathroom instead of her messy room, Carol thought of herself.

It wasn't as if she was bad person. She really wasn't. But she had standards and her standards were a priority, and she thought that everyone, her husband included, should know this about her. Like her hair and nails done a certain way. Her clothing bought from the right places. Also the address of her home, who saw it, and what sort of furniture was in it. Jake had never understood that. He would have gladly lived in a one-bedroom place with all old furniture had she not made him do what she wanted. Like that stuff he'd brought into her home.

"He'll just have to live with disappointment. I certainly have since I married him." Jake was just too.... Well, he was too nice. He was polite to everyone. Did everything he was supposed to in a timely manner, and when things weren't his way or she got upset with him, he just nodded and told her he was sorry. "Like sorry is going to cut it. He never gave me flowers or diamonds. For what I've had to endure, I should have been drenched in lovely things."

"Perhaps because of your spending he figured you had enough lovely things. You prevented him from doing a great many things, I'm thinking, just being the person that you are." She stared at her daddy as he entered the room and sat in the chair by her fireplace. "I've come to have a conversation with you. And for once, you're going to do as I tell you or there will be consequences."

"I don't think I care for your tone, Daddy. And Jake is the one that is going to have to face the consequences. I've been trying hard to get him to understand that I'm not going to give him a divorce." She made her way to the closet to find the perfect pair of shoes. "I'm going out to talk to Jake. He has been doing things to my house that I just don't care for."

"As you've done to mine? What is this mess, Carol? What have you done here?" She told him it was time for a new room. "No, this one is just fine, or it was. You're not going to do anything to this room because it no longer belongs to you."

"What does that mean?" He told her that she was too old to be living at home. "I'm working on that, Daddy. Didn't I just tell you that I was going to talk to Jake? He has had someone telling him that we need to divorce. I'm not going to allow that. Daddy, you should see the stuff he had coming in. Hideous."

"Carol, he's divorcing you and there is nothing I can do to stop it. I've called his father and explained it to him, but who knows what will come of that. You should move on. He has."

Carol just stared at her daddy, then asked him if he wanted her to be sad. "No. But I do think you need to come to the realization that he's not going to take you back. And as much as I hate to say it, I think it's for the best. For him anyway."

"Daddy, how can you say such a thing? I married him so that I could be his wife and get all the things I wanted and deserved." He asked her if she loved him. "What does that have to do with anything? He married me and that's the way I wanted it. We're going to get over this little bump in the road. I'm even going over there today to move back in. He'll be glad to see me once I get the house back to the way it was before."

"If you say so." Her daddy stood up, and that was when she noticed that he was looking old. "I've decided that I'm going to help him leave you. I know that you don't want to hear that, but I think you're not right for him. You never were. I love you dearly, Carol, but that man deserves better. It's taken me a long time to realize that, but you're not a nice person. And I'm not going to bail you out anymore. But before you go and take the furniture over there, you might want to check the locks on his home. I think you might be surprised that he's working on keeping you out completely. Also, your mother and I have talked it over, and you have thirty days to get your life together and out on your own. We'll not be taking you back to raise again. You're an adult. It's time you start acting like one."

After her daddy left, Carol decided that she'd have to work on getting him committed. There was something seriously wrong with her daddy. Not only was he not in his right mind about her and what she wanted, but he seemed to be thinking that she was the bad guy. Mom too. They were just too stupid to understand that she always got what she wanted.

Shaking her head at how sad it was, Carol decided that as soon as she was living in her home again, she was going to put this one on the market and look into nursing homes for her parents. Some place nice but not too expensive. She was going to need more money now to maintain two homes. Oh what the girls at the country club would think of her now, she thought. The owner of not one, but two houses.

The yard was being mowed by a service when she got to her home. There had never been a service when she was there, Jake telling her that they couldn't afford it. Well, they could now, and she was going to make sure he knew how disappointed she was that he'd waited until now to bring someone in.

It was nice, she thought, to not just have the lawn mowed, but to have the hedges trimmed as well as pretty flowers planted along the front of the house. She didn't care for the bland colors, but it would do for now. Going to the door, she tried to slide her key into the lock.

"Can I help you?" Carol turned to the man who spoke. He was dressed in the same outfit that the guy mowing was. "Mr. Winslow isn't home right now. He left me in charge of the place until he returns. And he never mentioned that anyone was coming by today. Sorry."

"I'm his wife. I've been away on some business. But it seems that my key doesn't work. If you're in charge, then you must have a key. I want you to let me in now. I have things I have to get taken care of. Oh, and I will need for you and a couple of those men out there to come in the house and drag out some furniture. Jake will take care of you when he gets here." He looked at the door then back at her. "I'm his wife, I told you. I need to get in there. I'm having my things delivered in an hour, and I need to make sure that the walls weren't painted over or harmed while I was gone."

"I know for a fact that the walls are in first-rate condition. There was a painting firm in yesterday and the day before. I think they redid the whole house, as a matter of fact." She was going to murder Jake when she saw him if he'd painted over the colors she picked out. "And Mr. Winslow told me specifically that I'm not to let you in, Carol."

"It's Mrs. Winslow to you. I've not given you permission to call me by my given name. And I'll tell Jake about this when he gets home. Open the door." He crossed his arms over his chest and stood there. "Did you hear me? Are you stupid? I want you to open this damned door right fucking now."

"No. I'm going to have to ask you to leave now, or I will call the police. They've been warned about you as well." Carol was furious, and drew back her hand to slap the man when he spoke again. "I'm not going to allow you to get away with hitting me, if that's where your mind is going. If you do, then I'm well within my rights to hurt you back. And I will. Also, in the event that you try and claim that I started this, I'd like to point out that there is a camera pointed right at us and it will show that you started it. So, it would behoove you to get out of here now before I call the police, as I've said to you once already."

Carol was tempted to see if he would really hurt her. She knew there were no cameras pointed at them either. Jake had told her numerous times that they lived in a good neighborhood and no one would bother them. Carol also knew that she was well within her rights to slap someone who treated her this way, but she wasn't sure that he was smart enough to know the rules. Carol looked around and saw that the other two workers, the guy with the mower and the other with trimmers of some sort, were staring at her as if they expected her to be hurt too.

"When my husband finds out how you're treating me, he's going to sue you and make sure that you all lose your jobs over this. He won't tolerate this sort of treatment to his wife." The man said nothing. "I'm going now, but not because you told me to. I have other things to do today. But you can bet that I'll be back and you will be sorry."

"All right." He moved to the side and her palm itched to hit him. Wound him badly, as a matter of fact. "Don't return, Carol. If you do, I'll consider it trespassing and I will call the cops the moment you step out of your car. You've been warned."

"We'll just see about that." He said nothing as she made her way to her car. Carol was trembling with anger. When Jake heard from her again, she was going to tell him how much she did not appreciate being treated this way.

On her way home she decided that she wasn't going to call the moving firm. Let that bastard deal with them when they got there. She hoped that they'd just dump the pretty things on the front lawn and be done with it. It would be a shame for it to be messed up like that, but she figured that Jake owed her new things for the way he'd been treating her. Calling her mom, she asked her to meet her for lunch. When she turned her down, Carol decided that everyone was going to pay for their treatment of her.

~~~

Jake was looking over a file, not even sure what he was reading because his mind was so preoccupied with other crap that it took him several moments to realize that his cell phone was ringing. Pulling it out, he nearly didn't answer since he had no idea who the number belonged to. But in the end, he said hello.

"It's Forrest. I need your help." Jake stood up, reaching for his jacket even as he continued. "I'm at Mercy and I've been hurt pretty badly, but I need for someone to come here and.... Could you just come here and sit with me? I hate to ask, but I'm...I'm having a difficult time of it right now."

"Of course. I'm on my way." He was telling his secretary where he was going as he headed out the door. "Are you all right? Do you need me to bring you anything? Call someone for you?"

"No. My dad hasn't spoken to me in years. My mom died about three years ago, so I'm pretty much alone." Jake told him he was sorry as he set up his phone on the holder to talk while he drove. "I wouldn't have called you at all but I have to tell you, I'm a little freaked out. Someone tried to kill me last night. On the property that surrounds my complex."

Jake paused in starting his car. "Was it Carol?" He had no idea why that would have popped into his head, but lately, and he more than likely had thought it before, he thought that Carol was off her noodle as Grandma said. "I know that she was pissed about the divorce paperwork, but there was no reason for her to try and hurt you."

"I think it was Thomas." Jake started the car and left the lot without asking. He wanted to, with all his heart, but it wasn't any of his business. Forrest laughing made him feel odd again. "It's more than over for us, but Thomas was my lover for a time. He was also a con artist. He took me for a bit, but when he tried to get into my bank account I realized just how bad it was. Does this make you not want to come here? I'd understand."

"I don't know enough about you to think that Thomas or anyone else is any of my concern." Which was true, but he felt something settle over him when Forrest told him it was over. "I'm on my way. And if you don't mind, I'd like to tell my grandma too. I know she thinks a great deal of you as well."

"I'd like that. Very much. Even after what I just told you, you're really still coming?" He told him he was. "All right then. They've got me in a room. If I could escape from here, I could shift and be all right. But I think, for now, this is the best thing. The wounds are going to go a long way in getting rid of the bastard. If I shift I'll be healed, and I have a feeling that no one would care any longer."

"What happened to you?" Forrest asked him if he could just tell him when he came in. "Of course. Are you sure that I can't bring you anything? Food? Coffee?"

"No. Just seeing you will be enough. Just having someone here with me will improve my mood greatly."

Jake told him he was only about ten minutes out. After he hung up, instead of calling his grandma right away, he thought about some of the things he'd looked up last night on the Internet.

Male on male sex was somewhat like having sex with a female, but not entirely. Even in his addled mind that made no sense, but he'd felt better after reading up on a few things. Not that he'd ever enjoyed sex with Carol, but he'd read about homosexual sex and had even gone so far as to watch a couple of videos that he'd found. He wasn't sure he'd be able to satisfy Forrest any better than he had his own wife, but he had watched enough to know that men seemed to have a better handle on sex than women did.

First of all, they touched a great deal. Like not just where you'd think to touch another person — the breasts, thighs, as well as their mouths — but men touched everywhere. The backs of knees, their feet. Nothing was left untouched or unloved. He shifted on his seat, thinking of how hard he'd come last night watching them.

And then there was how hard they seemed to come. Not just a release from their cock, but it radiated from their entire person. They shouted out with each release. Coming from their hearts, Jake had thought. It was a beautiful sight to behold.

It hadn't been his plan to get aroused by watching them. In fact, Jake had a hard time remembering the last time he'd been sexually excited. Not for a long while, at least. But then he'd watched the two men, who he thought were really in love, make love to each other. Like they had meant the very world to one another. Then when they both came, it was as if his entire body had been a part of it. His cock erupted twice, spilling out so much of his cum that he ached afterwards.

Jake had sat there, his cock still semi hard, his heart pounding and his breathing harsh, as he thought of what he'd just done. How much he'd enjoyed coming while watching what he'd just seen. Never once did he feel like it was wrong. Nor did he feel guilty over it. At one time he might have, he supposed. Carol would have found out and he would never have lived it down. She was good at making him feel like he was less than a person.

As he pulled into the parking lot to the hospital a few minutes later, he sat there for several minutes just thinking of Forrest. And some of the things he'd been able to find out from his friend who was also a shifter, though a wolf.

He'd told him that while he didn't know any homosexual shifters, he had heard of them. They were a rare breed, but not thought of negatively in their world as they were in the human one. Peter, his friend, had told him that they were more accepting of things like that, and rarely, if ever, were any issues with anyone's sexual preference ever brought up as they were in the human race.

"The only thing we care about is that you care for your other half. That you are good to each other and kind to the population in general." He also told him about cats, or what he knew. "Cats are a very different breed than we are. Not just because they're cats and we're canine, but I mean, wolves like to cuddle, hold each other as much as we can. Cats are the same, but they don't live with others. Not in packs. A pride, which is what it's called, they're more of a single male, his mate, and any children they might have. He can take on the role of leader to more should he want to, but — and this is only what I've heard not what I actually know — they tend to stay in smaller groups. Once they're old enough, they might live close but they don't live in a single dwelling."

Jake had wondered how that would work when he and Forrest got together, and it surprised him a little that such thoughts came into his mind. And now as that thought entered his head again, a permanency that he'd never thought of before, Jake got out of his car while calling his grandma.

She said that she'd be over later, once her bridge club was done, and bring them all dinner. He loved her for her forethought. Grandma also told him that she'd set up a meeting with Tyler Lane, but she wasn't sure what would come of it. Jake told her to be careful.

Entering Forrest's room, he was dismayed to think that he didn't get him flowers. There were a great many of them in the room, most of them with cards, some of them with small notes. Forrest told him it didn't matter, he was just glad to see him. He walked to the bed and leaned in to hug him. Jake wasn't sure that Forrest was going to hug him back, and when he did, he felt better, restored in some way, and thought that was exactly how he felt. Restored. He asked him how he was doing.

"I'm better now; thank you so much for coming in. Last night when they brought me here, I was sort of out of it. I don't know what I would have done if the wolf pack that roams around the land that I live by hadn't found me." The bandage across his forehead was dark with blood stains. "It's healed pretty much. But for appearances I have to pretend to be on my death bed."

"You should have had them call me. I would have come in to be with you. I'm not sure what I would have been able to do but to talk to you, but I would have been there for you." Forrest said he wasn't thinking right, just terrified. "We should have some sort of notes that come up to call each other when we're hurt. That way you don't have to go through this alone."

"I am alone, Jake. And have been for a very long time." He sounded so broken that it hurt Jake to hear it. "I'm sorry. I've been lying here for hours just thinking and feeling sorry for myself. You should have been here before, when I was crying like a small child. I never cry. But I'm feeling particularly whiny today."

"Well of course you are. You've been shot." He reached for Forrest's hand and was glad when he curled his fingers around his. "I've been thinking. About us. I mean a lot."

"And what have you figured out? I'm assuming that you've not decided to run to the hills." Jake shook his head. "I have to tell you something first. Before you tell me anything, I want you to think of what your parents will say. Hell, for that matter, what society will have to say. They'll not be kind to either of us."

"No, I've thought of that as well. Not a lot but some. My parents aren't happy with me anyway, for marrying Carol." Forrest laughed. "Yeah, I'm sure that they're going to be thrilled to no end when I tell them that I'm living with another man."

"Are you? Planning to live with me?" Jake asked him if he would have any trouble with moving in with him. "No, I won't. But again, people will talk. I think you'll even begin to have problems with the firm that you work for. To be honest, it's why I have my own practice. I didn't care for the way corporate America treats my kind."

"Yeah, about that. I'm leaving my firm. As of this morning, as a matter of fact. I gave my notice in the form of a letter and email. I was up for partnership but was passed over again. Wendell, the guy that is in charge of hours and how that is set up, told me that I'd never be promoted, not the way I work. Then it was confirmed by the guy who is in charge of the hiring. They like having me just where I am because I work a lot of hours." Jake nodded. "I'm going to hang out my own shingle, and if that doesn't work, I'll figure something out."

"Work with me. We could be partners." Jake said that wasn't what he was going for. "Maybe not, but we could make it work. And with both of us bringing in hours, we could save some money too."

"I don't really need to work." Forrest said he knew that as well. "I guess you would. My grandda, he left me a large chunk of money when he passed away. And Grandma told me that she's leaving her money to me as well. It was a nice bit of cash. Carol never knew, of course. Had she known, I don't think I could easily say that about not working. She would have drained the pot and I'm betting that it still might not have been enough for her."

"No, she would have taken you to the cleaners and then stepped over your corpse had she any idea of your worth. But she's having her own set of troubles." Forrest told him how he'd talked to her dad just yesterday. "Her parents have given her a month to get her affairs in order and get out. I guess her mom wants her out now, but they said a month is all they'll give her. I think we can get off with no sort of alimony to her if we can show that she's not trying to make her way in this world and never has. This is a no fault state, lucky for her, or we'd have her paying you. But as it is, I don't think you'll have to fork out any more than necessary to end this."

"When I heard about the abortions, it was all I could do not to hunt her down and ask her about it. But I figured it wouldn't do me any good. She'd just figure out a way to turn it so that it was my fault. Carol would never admit to being wrong about anything." He related the story about her coming to the house today. "This guy, Mark, who works for Grandma, was at the house with his crew, working on the yard when she showed up. He said that just after she left, the moving company called, asking for directions to my house. Mark explained to them that she no longer lived at that residence and that they should take it to her home. Her parents' home. Mark said the guy was still laughing when he hung up. I guess Carol was none too nice to him when she made the arrangements in the first place."

"I tried to get them to take it to her earlier this week, but that fell through. She didn't put it in her name but her father's, since he was being billed for the place." Forrest grinned. "I think this is so much better. You refusing the delivery will say a lot to her, and her father will be pissed when it gets to her. Damn, but I wish I could have seen her face when she was turned away. That is not a nice woman."

"I have it on my computer. I set up some security cameras a few days ago so I could keep an eye on the place with her locked out. It wouldn't have surprised me to find out that she'd broken in or something." Forrest said he'd thought the same thing. "You have no idea how content I am that she's out of my life. No one does. I'm almost giddy with it."

They talked about this and that, nothing about whatever came next for them nor about Carol. Jake finally asked him about Thomas and why Forrest thought it was him who had hurt him. At first he wasn't sure he was going to answer, but he finally did.

"I didn't actually see him there, but I could smell him. And I heard laughter. He brays like a jackass, and I knew it was him. Then when my head exploded in pain, I just passed out." Jake nodded, understanding that Forrest would be able to catch this other man's scent simply because they had been lovers. "I was running off steam, I guess, and not really paying attention to what was going on around me. I was on property that I thought was safe...it's not much but all I had, and figured I was safe."

"What would drive him to resort to trying to kill you? Or was it simply he wanted you to hurt?" Forrest said he didn't know. "What do you plan to do about it? I'm assuming that you have something going on in that head of yours."

"I do. I wasn't sure that I wanted to, not at first. It's sort of embarrassing to have someone try to take advantage of you in these sort of situations. But I've thought it over, and since I know there are others out there, ones that he's scammed as well, I'm going to go all out to get him off the streets. Or at least his name out so that others can be aware of him before they're taken." Jake asked him if he could help. "I was actually hoping you could. I read over your file, and you have some pretty good contacts with people that get jobs done. I don't want him killed, mind you, but I do want others safe."

"It would be my pleasure. And maybe if word gets out, others will come forth and testify against him. I mean, I know it would be hard, but if just one person is safe then it's worth it." Forrest said he agreed. "I can't imagine what sort of things you've had to put up with over your lifetime. I know something about your dad. Grandma told me what a prick he is."

"He is all that and more. When I first came out, he told me that he'd pay for me to be fixed. I wasn't sure what he meant at first, thought he wanted me to get help or something. No, he wanted me to be castrated—his words, not mine—so that I'd not breed any more of my kind into the world. My mom took it in stride. She told me not long before she died that she knew all along, and was glad that I was embracing myself. I nearly wet myself when she said that. Embracing myself like I was finally coming to know me. I miss her every day."

"I was never close to my parents. I had a brother, but he was killed in a biking accident when I was about twelve. Benny was two years younger me, and I think that my mom and dad figured that I should have been there for him." Forrest told him he was sorry. "It's all right. I mean, I tell myself that. But when Benny was killed I was at a school function. I think some sort of debate team or something. My dad said that had I been home, I could have been watching out for him. Mom just told me she was disappointed, in between sobbing how much she'd lost and that no one would ever understand it. I was never sure if she meant that I hadn't been killed or that I wasn't with Benny when he was. And they hated Carol."

Both of them fell silent after that. Jake wanted to ask him again if he was all right, but could almost feel that he was. The television was on, muted since neither of them seemed to be paying attention to it. When Forrest squeezed his hand, Jake turned to him.

"I was wondering; would you mind very much if I kissed you?" Jake felt his heartrate triple. It was not that he was afraid of a kiss, but he was nervous about where it might lead. Or for that matter, where he wanted it to lead. "If you don't want to, I understand."

"No, it's not that. I don't know how." Forrest asked him what he meant. "I kissed Carol on our wedding day, but not since. Not anyone but Grandma. I know that sounds really stupid, but I never really wanted to be with her. Not sexually, nor even as a friend. Not that she wanted any more from me apparently, but I've never really enjoyed sex or kissing."

"Well, it sounds like you're due." Jake stood up, his body aching for something more than he knew to name. And when he leaned toward Forrest, making sure not to hurt him in anyway, Jake moaned when Forrest pulled his head closer and touched his lips to his.

CHAPTER 5

Forrest tried not to be greedy. He'd wanted to pull him into his arms and bed since he'd walked in the door and sat down. He'd nearly cried when Jake took his hand in his like he'd been doing it forever. And now, right now, he was close enough for him to touch everywhere he wanted. But he didn't. Not yet.

The kiss was soft, not hungry like he wanted. But this was better, Forrest thought. It was an exploration for them both. And even though Forrest wanted this man with all that he was, he also knew that Jake was still new to their relationship. Even to this lifestyle.

When Jake lifted his head and rested his forehead on his, Forrest wanted to ask him if he was all right. But his tongue was tied up in knots, just as his belly was. So when Jake leaned in and kissed him again, Forrest couldn't have held back his need if he'd had to.

Hunger. It was as ripe as the roses in the vases near them.

Even as fragrant. Forrest touched his hand to his chest, just to make sure that this was real, when Jake moaned. It served as an invitation to him. Forrest wanted more, he wanted it all. Pulling him closer, almost over him, Forrest slid his hand down his chest to his pants and cupped Jake's cock. He moaned when he felt not just his length, but how hard he was as well. Jake pulled away and looked down to where his hand was.

"I've thought of nothing else but you touching me like this." Forrest wanted to reach into his pants, free his cock, and hold him, but was trying his best to take this slow enough where they were not fucking on a hospital bed. "The thought of being in your mouth makes me hurt."

"Christ." He nearly tore Jake's pants off him in his haste. Forrest needed him. Wanted to pull him up over him and let him come all over his body. As soon as he had Jake free, he slid his hand up and down his shaft as Jake moved his sheets out of the way. "I want to come on you, mark you."

"Yes. Oh yes, I would love that too." When his own cock was freed, he watched Jake's hand slide up and down him, felt him rock into his own palm as he fucked him with his hand. "I can suck you, right? I need to taste your cock."

If he answered him, he wasn't sure. Jake pulled from him and leaned over his body and took him deep into his mouth. Forrest cried out, the heat of Jake's mouth almost too hot. He was as close to coming as he'd ever been when Jake moved his head down to his balls and suckled one into his mouth.

"I've never done this before. Tell me if I hurt you." Forrest said that he would as he watched him lick his length before taking his crown in his mouth again before looking at him. "I love the taste of you. When you come, will I be able to taste all of you?"

His cock felt tight, his balls pulled up close to his body, hot with cum. As Jake sucked, bobbing his head up and down over him, licking his length when he could, Forrest rocked upward, feeling the tight muscles at the back of Jake's throat. Forrest curled his fingers into his hair to help guide him. Really, it wasn't so much as guiding him, he realized, as he was just holding on. It was both heaven and hell having Jake doing these things to him.

Forrest was close to coming…he could feel it as the ecstasy ran over his body. He wanted to bring Jake as well, show him heights that they could both enjoy together, but the bed wasn't cooperating and they had to be extra quiet. Even as Jake slid his hands over his balls again, cupping them in his fingers, Forrest wanted to cry out, release in a way that everyone within miles would know that he had his mate. Then Jake slid his finger up under his ass and into his tight hole.

Forrest came hard. Stars danced in front of his eyes. The pounding of his heart sounded like drums beating to a rhythm that he'd never heard before but loved. As his balls filled again, his cock stretching out longer, he felt Jake fucking him, his fingers making him think of silk sheets, hot summer nights sleeping with the window open, and commitment all at once. Then he came a second time and Forrest cried out, even the pillow over his mouth doing nothing to stop the sound from echoing around the room.

Aftershocks made him ache. Forrest felt his heart not just pounding but coming alive at the same time. Pulling Jake to him, his mouth still smeared with his cream, he kissed him, showing him as best he could how he felt. Then he reached for his cock.

"Come on me." Jake nodded, holding onto the mattress above his head as he held him in his hand. "Christ, come all over me so I can come again."

"I'm so close. I need to come now." Forrest slid his hand faster up and down his shaft, using the cum that streamed there as a lubricant. He wanted to see his face, watch him as he came for the first time with him. And when he threw back his head and cried out, Forrest held his own cock as he came yet again.

He was spent and felt wonderful, like he'd run a marathon and had the best sleep he'd ever had at the same time. And when Jake leaned to him, laying his head on his chest, he held him there, feeling like the weight of the world was off his back. Forrest was in love. For the first time in his life, he was truly in love.

"I never thought it would be that way." Forrest waited, knowing that Jake was going to tell him that he was sickened by what they'd just done; or worse yet, that he'd not really enjoyed it that much. "I have to sit. My legs are wobbly and I feel slightly lightheaded."

After they both straightened up their clothing, Forrest felt his anger start to take him. He'd just had the best sex of his life with a man that he loved, and now he was going to leave him. But before he could speak, Jake started talking. It took him several moments before he was able to understand.

"I saw these two men on the Internet having sex. It seemed too wonderful for them. I mean, like they were really in love and all. I thought, no one would feel that way about me. I'd be lucky if you didn't turn me away the first time I touched you. I'm not in the best of shape. I've been thinking about working on my body, but I've just been so down lately that I've let some things slide. Mostly how I look. Mostly because of Carol, but I've also been so worried at work about things. What was going to happen if they picked someone over me? Now I don't have to worry about that any more, but it seems that something else would pop into my head to worry over. Then there is the—" Forrest said his name and nearly laughed when Jake's mouth snapped closed. "I'm nervous. Babbling about stupid things. But I'm terrified, if you want to know the truth, that you're going to tell me that this was a mistake. That you really aren't my mate or something like that."

"No, I won't turn you away. And that was the best sex I've ever had. I never expected it to happen...not between us, I guess." Jake grinned like a kid. "I'm nervous too, if you want the truth. I was sure when you sat down that you'd tell me the same thing. It wasn't for you or something like that. Then when you took my hand in yours it was like you were saying to me that it was okay with you, this thing between the two of us. Did you really watch a video of two men?"

"Yes. I got to thinking how I knew nothing about sex with another man. And when they were coming, the two of them climaxing like they did, I did as well." His face turned a deep shade of red. "All I could think about afterwards was how fulfilling it had been. And a huge turn on. Not watching strangers, but that I had come so hard."

"Coming like this, with you, you have no idea how good

it felt." Jake said he had a pretty good idea. "Well, I guess you would. I can't believe...I guess I expected we'd wait or that we'd take it slower."

"I think that I've been taking things slow my whole life." Forrest watched Jake as he got up to pace the room. "I thought about us all night. Not just sexually, though that played a big part of it, but just in other things. Getting to know each other, being with you. Did you know that when we had that dinner together the other night, I was so relaxed that I slept straight through the night? I never do that. Something always disturbs my sleep at least twice."

"We'll still need to take this slow. I know that I don't care what other people think, but we both have a career to think about, as well as our families. I don't think mine could hate me any more than they already do, but there is Carol." Jake nodded as he continued to pace. "Your grandma will act as if this was her entire idea and that she invented homosexuality."

"She might. I don't know what I would have done without her over the years. She's been a rock in my life." Forrest told him that she was for him as well. Jake stopped moving and looked at him. "What do we do now? Do we keep meeting in secret? Do we go to out of town hotels to be together? I don't want to, but I'm not sure that just moving in together won't cause us some problems, like you said."

"I think, for the time being, that we *try* and take things slowly. Your divorce will be messy enough without the added drama of us." Jake agreed. "We can meet in my offices. Or at your house. But we have to be careful. Just for now."

"I agree. And if Carol gets wind of this, it will be spread

all over the place. That she was the injured party in this. And I can see her making up stories that she caught us together in some compromising position as well." Forrest had thought that as well. "All right. We'll do like this, to save us both. But in the meantime, I'd very much like to take you up on that partnership. If you still think we can work together."

"Oh yes. More than ever. I'm not sure how much actual work we'll get done, but I think we can make a go of it." They were both still laughing when Jenna came into the room.

"Good, I'm glad that the two of you aren't going to let a little gossip change who you are." She began pulling thick sandwiches out of a picnic basket as she continued. "By the way, I've spoken to my son. He is not any happier with me than he is with you. I told him that Carol was a bitch and that you were divorcing her. Nothing more, but I would expect him to talk to you. He seems to think you're a fool and are going to cost him money over this. I haven't any idea how he's come to that conclusion, but he's always been a bastard in my book. I wanted to tell him your bed was your concern now, but I didn't. I can hold a secret no matter how much I want to spill the beans. Especially to him. Who would have thought I could have had such a son? Not me, that's for sure."

Forrest thought that his life from now on was going to be epic. And happy. There was no doubt that he'd have to keep on his toes with these two; and more than that, he'd never be lonely again. Now if he could just get home to show Jake how to properly make love he'd be content. And the rest of the world could go straight to fucking hell.

~~~

Thomas made his way to the bar he frequented. It was also the place where he did his best work. He had things he needed to get done soon, but without the funds to do so, he was at a standstill. Three men, all of them dressed in business suits and drinking beer, caught his attention as soon as he walked in. They were as good as any place to start, he thought. Men like them wouldn't know what hit them when he started his little game.

Smiling, he thought about Forrest. He was as good as dead now. It had been his plan only to wound him. But the longer he'd had to sit there, waiting for the prick to come home, the more violent his plans had become.

Forrest had been royally pissed when he'd found out about the little things that Thomas had taken from him. And rightly so, he supposed. Thomas had had a good laugh over each piece of shit he'd taken every time he'd gone to his fence. And how he'd been able to take about five grand worth of his shit before he noticed.

Little things really, nothing that was big enough to be glaring, but take them he had. Then the fucking bank had ruined it all for him, too soon for him to get the real payoff. Pictures of them together for blackmail, cleaning out the account that he knew was right there for the taking. Thomas wanted to find that guy and make him pay as well. But Forrest had called in a couple of favors. Thomas saw that the banker and his family were being watched over too closely for his tastes; he'd been jumped and left him alone. For now, anyway.

He was sure it had been Forrest that had done that too. There wasn't any conversation when he'd been shadowed after leaving the bar that night. Just three men shoving him into a dark alley then beating him to shit. They left him there, curled up in a ball and bleeding. It was what had prompted him into going after Forrest and making him pay for all that he'd lost.

They'd broken his arm in two places, as well as several ribs, so it had been hard on him, going out to the field where Forrest went on occasion. But the worse part of it was, they'd messed up his face. Thomas took pride in how his face looked. Right now he was sporting nineteen stitches in his lip, forty over his left eye, and thirteen along his cheek. He was a mess and he knew it.

Vinny, the bartender, knew him and set a tall glass of what was basically colored water in front of him. It was nothing more than water with cherry juice and a squeeze of lime in it. But it resembled a tall drink and that was what he was going for. Props, he called them, to look the part of a man who knew his way around a bar.

When one of the men that he had targeted came to the bar for drinks, Thomas nodded. He wasn't going to move in just yet. As far as he could tell, these men were in for a while and he was going to take his time to peel them off from the pack, so to speak. There were three of them, and all he could think about was the other night when he'd been hurt. Safety in a single man, not a trio of them. Though the thought of the four of them together made his dick stretch.

"How you doing?" The man only nodded, saying that he was fine. As he moved away, taking his beers with him, Thomas motioned for Vinny. "I need your help again. I'll give you all the cash they have on them for some help separating them for me."

"Nah, I'm done with you." Thomas thought he was kidding and told him that he'd give him the goods if he'd put them in the glasses. "No, seriously. I'm done doing this work for you. Ain't worth the money."

"You can't be done with me. Damn it, we have a good thing going here." Vinny just shrugged. "What happened? The money not good enough for you now, or do you have another partner in this? The boss, he giving you shit again? I told you I'd help you out. I can send a little more your way if you need it." Vinny told him it wasn't that. "Then what? You can't just leave me hanging, buddy. I need you."

"Ever hear of a firm by the name of Winslow and Winslow?" Thomas said that he'd not had the pleasure. "I hadn't either until yesterday. This guy rolls on in here and tells me straight up if I help you in any way, even if it's to lend you a quarter to make a police call, he'd come back here and shut me down so fast that I won't even have the cash from the register. And for some reason I don't think he was talking about the bar, but me. I don't need that kind of shit coming my way. I have a family."

"That's bullshit. Why does he give a shit if you help a man out? Not to mention, how the fuck did he find out? You talking again, Vinny?" He said that he wasn't but the guy knew things. "What sort of things? I'm betting it was that lover of yours who told if you didn't. There is no way he'd know anything unless someone shared shit."

"Wasn't that. But he knew the drug that you gave me to put in the drinks of the patrons you wanted to hit. That's what he called them too, patrons. He said that you came in here, targeted a man or two, then I'd drug them. Then we'd take them out back, fuck them a little, then we'd leave them for the rats to pick over." Vinny looked around as if he expected this guy to pop out of the woodwork. "Then he showed me pictures. Of us. You and me beating the shit out of one of these guys then taking their goods. I don't need any shit, Thomas. And I can't lose my job. I need this thing."

Vinny moved away from him as if he was afraid of catching some disease. This wasn't right. Who the fuck did this guy think he was, messing with his livelihood? He was going to have a talk with this firm and see what the hell their problem was. Pulling out his phone to find out what he could, he looked up the company of Winslow and Winslow.

They were an investment group. A man and woman owned the place, more than likely fat rich fucks that hated gays as much as most of the world. Jenna and Jake Winslow were out to change the world, the column said about them. They were making a difference in a great many lives, and helping the underprivileged as well as the downtrodden.

"Fuck that shit." As he skimmed through the rest of the article that was dated last year, he wondered if they were the ones that had had him beaten up. "More than likely hired some shit to do it for them. Hell of a way they help the underprivileged, by taking their jobs from them."

Thomas tried twice more to get Vinny to help him. Not even the waitress, who he knew needed the cash, would turn his way when he said her name. Damn it, this was just stupid. He needed the cash these pricks had on them. And perhaps a few charges on a couple of their cards too. A man had to eat, didn't he?

When the second guy in the group made his way to the bar, he looked right at him. Thomas felt his neck hairs dance and his body go sweaty hot to ice cold in a heartbeat. There was something very scary about the way he was staring at him.

"You're Thomas Simpson, aren't you?" He had no choice but to answer him. When he nodded, the man laughed. "Yeah, we thought so. Are you having trouble scoring there, Tommy boy? Are you finding it hard to get someone to let you fuck them over? You might want to find a different profession. One that might let you live just a little longer."

"You think you know something? Well, I like what I do, and I'm pretty damned good at it too. So fuck off." The man said nothing but reached into his suit pocket, and that was when Thomas saw the gun. It wasn't one of those little cheap pieces of shit that he had sold out of the back of his car before either. This one was meant for business, not just show. "You have a gun? Why? You're supposed to be this big bad vamp, right? What do you want?"

"To kill idiots I don't want to get close to. As for what I want? Well, now that's a very powerful word there, want. I want you to die, but I'm not to touch you unless I have to protect myself. Are you going to give me a reason to touch you, Tommy boy?" He shook his head. "Too bad. So since you won't give me what I want, then I'm going to tell you what I need for you to do. Leave. Not just this bar, but this town. Just get in that piece of shit car you have and get the fuck out of town. Not that you'll have any better luck with your scam once you do go, but you might not be killed if we don't find you here again."

"I didn't do a damned thing to you. You have no right to order me to leave here." When the man straightened up, his body just growing taller as he did so, Thomas felt his balls tighten to his body. The man was fucking huge. "Don't hurt me."

"Why not? You hurt men all the time, don't you?" He nodded, again not able to keep himself from doing so. It was like he couldn't lie to him. And when he smiled, Thomas fell off the back of the stool he was sitting on and backed up to the wall. "I can see that we understand each other now. You know that as a vampire of some age, I can find your skinny ass wherever I want and whenever I need to. You might also keep in mind that I have some pretty powerful friends, and I can call on them with just a breath of air to end your miserable life."

The vampire moved toward him, slowly. He stared at his face too, like he was memorizing every detail about it for future reference. When he had him pressed to the wall, his body hurting as picture frames and other things behind him bit into his skin, Thomas wanted to look away, but he couldn't. The vampire had him. Captured him with his gaze, he thought it was called.

"Who sent you after me?" The man laughed, the sound of it like nails on a chalkboard to him. Not that his laughter wasn't full of humor, but to Thomas, it sounded just like that. "I deserve to know who sent you."

"Do you? I don't think you do. However, I will tell you this...." He was lifted up by the man, one hand to his throat was all it took. "You touch anyone again, for any reason, and I will not just end your sad life, but I will take great pleasure in tearing you into pieces so small that no one will find you. Even if there was a soul out there that would give a fuck you were dead."

Thomas staggered home. He wasn't entirely sure how he'd gotten there, but bits and pieces of himself falling and tumbling around on the sidewalks were a part of his recollections. Once he thought he'd been held at knife point, but he wasn't quite sure of that either. Things weren't just fuzzy for him, but they fluctuated between outright fear and blank spaces of time.

His first complete thought was how, sitting on his lumpy couch with his pants down around his ankles, he'd come to be in this state of undress. Thomas wasn't sure why or how it had happened, but he was half dressed and his head was pounding. Pulling his pants up as he made his way to the bathroom, he thought of what had happened in the bar. A vampire had threatened him.

Not that he didn't believe in such beings. He knew a great many shifters. Vampires, however, were animals that he left alone. They were not ones to fuck with, he'd learned the hard way. And in addition to being bad assed, they also had a long memory on shit that most people would just ignore. But not a vampire.

As he kicked off his pants and made his way to the shower, he thought of the shit that had gone down. He'd been threatened. By a vampire, no less. And who the fuck were these people, the Winslows, and what business was it of theirs what he did in his free time? It wasn't like he was hurting anyone. Then he thought of Forrest.

"Okay, so I killed him. But he drove me to it." Thomas

stared at his reflection in the mirror as he turned right then left, looking at his body. He was battered and bruised. His body had more cuts and sores on it than he'd had in his entire life up until now. "He should have been glad to have someone like me in his miserable life. And so what if there were a few things missing from his place? It's not like he didn't have a ton of money to replace them."

Money that he hadn't been able to cash in on. Thomas had known that Forrest, as a lawyer, would have a lot of it. Hell, the man didn't even own a house or a really nice car. There had to be millions of bucks just waiting there for him to collect on, but some fucking banker had gotten in his way of that. Just like this vampire had.

The shower wasn't nearly as long as he'd wanted. The hot water always ran out long before he was finished up, and that pissed him off more. As he was getting dressed, thinking more and more about the fucking vamp, he knew just what he was going to do. Go out to the field and piss on Forrest's rotten head.

Thomas thought as far as plans went, this one was the best he'd ever come up with. And he was going to tell that vampire next time he saw him to fuck off too. He was his own man, not a pussy like Forrest was.

CHAPTER 6

The ride to his home wasn't that long, but Jake was sort of nervous. He was bringing Forrest to his home for the first time, and he wanted things to be perfect. Not that he'd have any trouble changing whatever he didn't like—the house was pretty much still empty—but he was still nervous all the same.

The moment he pulled into the drive, he wanted to turn around and leave. His parents had finally decided to come around for some reason. Jake supposed now that he was divorcing Carol they figured it was time.

"Your parents, I take it?" He said that it was. "Well, how do you want to play this? That I'm recouping at your house? Or that you and I are old college friends and I'm hanging with you for a little while? I'm okay with that. We're still figuring this out."

"Would you mind? For now?" Forrest said it would be his pleasure to help out. "Thank you so much. I'm not sure what they'd do if they knew I was taking you here to have sex with you in every room of the house. Not that it's any of their business, but I just don't want to have to deal with them today."

Forrest laughed. "You do know how to cut to the chase, don't you? Why don't you stand up to them, Jake? I know that you have it in you." He said they scared him to death. "Yeah, I can understand that. But you think this is going to go badly, don't you?"

"Yes. My mom is going to be all hurt and start crying, as she always has. I have no idea why, but she can play the martyr better than any woman that I know. My dad is going to keep telling me he told me so, or something like that. Yes, he did say not to marry Carol, but then he said that I had to. Like I was twelve or something. Then he didn't come to the wedding, telling me that he wasn't going to be a party to my mistakes." Forrest said he should just not speak to them. "I'm not sure I can even do that. I would love to, but I'm not sure that I have that much in the way of balls."

"Here's what you do. Just think of what your grandma would say and then say that. She can cut to the end of a problem better than most attorneys I have had the unpleasant experience of working with." He stared at Forrest. "Or not. I'm just saying, the man I see now is not the one that nearly raped me in the hospital yesterday."

Grinning, Jake got out of the car. He didn't feel like the man he'd been before that either. Jake was still a little backward on things, like the nurse telling him off when he suggested to her that she not try and tear Forrest's head off when she was helping him dress. Or when the doctor had told him to hire a nurse for the man. Jake knew that Forrest was nearly healed and would be completely back to new as soon as he was able to shift. He was extremely protective of the man, and was willing to go to bat for him like he'd never wanted to do with Carol.

"Jake. We were wondering if you were ever going to get out and greet us. This is no way to treat guests." It was on the tip of his tongue to tell his father that guests weren't family, but didn't. "Who is this you have here? We didn't think you'd be entertaining so soon. No matter. I wish to talk to you about this divorce you think you're going to get. I want you to call whoever you have contacted and tell them you've made a terrible mistake. You have, you know. Winslow men do not hide from their duties to their family. No matter how much of a disappointment you are to us."

"Am I a disappointment to you, Father? I've always thought that, but really, I never understood why. Maybe you can explain that to me. And how, after all this time, you think you can order me around like I'm a child again." He felt his confidence grow as he held Forrest upright and heard him laugh. "What you doing here, Father? I thought you said you'd never darken my doorway again."

"I came to offer you our advice, and you will take it, Jake. I don't think you've thought of the ramifications of what this will do to your family. You'll need a steady hand in getting this cleared up now that you think to throw away your marriage like it was nothing but an old rag. I'm here to convince you to reconsider this nonsense. There will be talk, you know, and I don't think that your reputation could withstand it." Forrest stumbled a little and fell against his father. "Steady there. This

103

is a new suit."

"Father, he's been injured, and you're acting like your suit is more important than someone's health." His father pointed out how much the suit had cost. "I'm sure that you don't mean that your suit is more important than my friend. As for the talk, I really don't give a shit, not anymore. I'm divorcing Carol and there is nothing in this world that you can do to convince me otherwise."

"What is wrong with you today, Jake? This show of temper is not at all the way I would like to see you behaving. You should be ashamed of yourself, talking to me like that. Carol needs you." Jake wasn't surprised by the change of subject, or that he was going to be the bad guy in this now that he'd questioned his father. He looked at Forrest as he got him to the couch, and laughed when he winked at him. "Jake, I should like a word with you, in private. You've got some explaining to do about this thing that you're trying to do to Carol."

"Trying to do to Carol? I haven't any idea what you mean." He let out a long breath, then thought fuck it. His father wasn't ever going to treat him any differently whether he was divorced or not. "Are you speaking of the divorce? That's a done deal, Father. She had several abortions, did you know that? None of them were mine, but she had to get rid of the children so that there'd be no evidence of what she was doing. And one day a few weeks ago, I came home to an empty house. Not just that she was gone, but she took every piece of furniture, every picture off the wall, and even the food in the cabinets. Do you know why? Because I cut off her spending."

"A woman needs a hobby. You shouldn't have done that.

Give her what she wants and perhaps you can get on with your lives together. I suggest that you reinstate her cards, or whatever you need to do, and let her come home." He looked around the room, sparse to say the least, but Jake liked that they were his things. "This furniture in here? Is it someone's castoffs? Have you no sense of taste? At least when your wife was here, you had a nice place to come visit."

"How the hell would you know? You never once came here in all the time we've been married." His mother started sobbing. "Now what?"

"Oh Jake, you've embarrassed me so much with this. Did you know that the woman who does my hair said that you had a servant tell Carol to get off your porch? The neighbors are more than likely thinking that we've raised you wrong. How could you do this to me?" Jake said nothing but looked at Forrest. At the slight shake of his head, Jake knew that this would be a terrible time to bring him up and just why he was there. "Jake, we want you to stop this nonsense right now. You and her, you might not have been suited, and we did tell you that, but you can't do this to me. To your family. You have to listen to your father and make this right. We're looking bad with what you've done."

His father was nodding then, as if his mother had it all worked out. "That's right. I will make a few calls, have this entire thing stopped as of this moment. There is no reason for you to make it public that you've made a terrible choice. And once this is completed, things back the way they should be, you'll do just what is expected of you and life will go on." Jake looked at the doorway when his father did. Grandma stood there with her back stiff. "Mother, you're to stay out of this. This is no concern of yours. I don't want to have to listen to your side of this right now."

"It's none of yours either, Jacob. Nor is it any of yours, Trina." Grandma came into the room as she had thousands of times before, and sat on the couch next to Forrest. "I'm so glad to see that they released you, dear. How is your poor head? Did you fill out a police report?"

It was all it took to get his mother going again. "Police? Oh no, you can't have the police here as well. Whatever will the people that live next to you think? Oh Jake, this is getting worse and worse all the time. Just call Carol up and tell her you've had a change of heart. And send this young man on his way; you don't need any more scandal right now. The police will need to make a report, and there will be filings and such. Oh my, this is terrible, just terrible for us."

"I don't want any scandal either, but it appears that I'm going to get it. I'm perfectly content right now with the way things are. Carol is not coming back. I'm not going to give her any more access to my money, and I most certainly will not allow her to continue to ruin my life." He looked around the room much as his father had. "I love this room. And the other furniture that I went and picked out on my own is more suited to me than anything that Carol had here. If you don't care for it, then that's fine. I didn't invite you here, and don't expect to in the future."

"You need us here. We're going to keep together on this as a family so that nothing else tarnishes our name. You've nearly ruined it with this stupidity already. Jake, you just aren't smart enough to—"

Jake had had enough and stood up. "It's time you left." Jake watched his father's face, the moment he realized what he'd said to him. "I don't want nor did I ask for your counsel on my life. Get out of here. And don't come back. This is my home, my life, and my mistakes. And as of this moment, I'm taking control of it again and doing things my way. Not yours. Not Carol's, and certainly not the way the neighbors think I should. If they even had an opinion one way or the other."

"We have things to discuss over this. You are not getting a divorce, Jake. I've told you that. It's a tarnish on our good name. Damn it, you cannot mean to kick us out." Jake said that was exactly what he was doing, and that he'd not asked them for help in the first place. "I will not tolerate you treating me this way. I am your father."

"So you are. And that sobbing mess is my mother. But really, other than DNA, we have nothing in common. I'd very much like it if you were to go. And even if you don't want to go, I can find someone to kick your asses out if it comes to that." His mother started wailing at the top of her lungs. "Enough."

His voice had been strong and loud. So much so that his mother stopped wailing and stared at him with fat tears rolling down her cheeks, and his father looked as if he'd hit him in the back of the head. It was invigorating as well as empowering. Then he looked over at his grandma.

She started clapping her hands. Forrest laughed. It might have been comical, what with his parents standing there looking at him as if they hadn't a clue who he was. Jake felt.... Well, he felt like he could take on the world and come out the winner.

His father seemed to have shaken off his stupor and looked ready to do battle again. "You'll regret this. As soon as your business starts to suffer, you'll regret this. See if I'm not right." Jake said nothing, knowing that on a level that his father didn't know yet, he might well fail. "I'm not going to step in this time and help you out."

"When did you ever, Father? When was it you might have dirtied your hands for me?" His father said he didn't care for his tone. "Well, I don't care for the way you're treating me either. As I have said to you, several times now, I'd very much like for you to leave."

His father turned to Grandma. "This is all your doing. You never did have a bit of sense of decorum when it came to being a Winslow." Grandma stood up and looked at her only son. "Just look at you. Standing there as if none of it bothers you. What would your husband say to all this?"

"My husband? You mean your father? And just to clarify things, I was a Winslow long before you were. So was your father. And my James would be right proud, I think." His father said thank you. "Not of you, dolt, but Jake. It's about time he stood up to you. I don't know if you're aware of this or not, but you're a bully. Plain and simple, you're a mean bully. And I think it's about time that Jake did leave the tramp. Carol is nothing more than a money grubbing bitch that should have been put in her place about the time you should have been. How something as cold and heartless as you came from us is beyond me. The only redeeming thing is that I have Jake to console my old soul."

"Mother, you'll not talk to me this way either. I'm a man of worth, not some sniveling boy you can talk into doing whatever you want." She asked him if he meant Jake. "Yes. You've been talking in his ear since he was old enough to walk. I should have put a stop to it then. But I thought...well, I had hoped that you'd not be around as much."

"You mean you thought I'd die and leave you to your life?" Jake's father nodded, then looked at Jake. Grandma laughed, long and hard. That brought his attention back to his mother. "I have news for you, Jacob, I'm going to be around a lot longer than you can imagine. I've been having fun with a certain vampire, who assures me that should I want, he can make me live forever. And you know what? I might just do it. Just to torment you."

His father and mother left after that. No more words were spoken, not if you didn't count his mother lamenting about how she wouldn't be able to show her face again. How her country club would cancel their membership. Even going so far as to say that they might have to move to another city, or even state, to get the stain of this off them.

His father just glared at him and his grandma. Jake might have thought it was funny, but he hated stress and it was making his belly turn in all sorts of directions, none of them good. And as soon as the door was closed on their visit, Jake ran to his bathroom to be sick.

~~~

"He's never done that before." Forrest looked over at Jenna when she spoke. "Not once has he ever stood up to anyone, and especially not his own parents. I think you might be good for him. It certainly made me feel wonderful to see him do that.

He's needed it for a long while now."

"I'm pretty sure right about now, he's thinking I'm the worst thing that has ever happened to him." Jenna laughed and said she doubted that. "I do believe that his dad is worse than mine. My dad was very vocal about how he was going to disown me once I came out, but his dad, I'm betting when or if Jake ever tells him about us, he's going to come here with a shotgun."

"Oh no, not Jacob. He'd never get his own hands dirty when it came down to it. He'd hire someone to off you." Forrest was so shocked that it took him several minutes to realize that she was kidding. Or at least he hoped so. "Besides, he'd be too worried about how that might tarnish his good name to have someone in his family killed. The repercussions would be hard to get over. You know, Forrest, I never realized until this very moment that I raised an asshole."

Forrest laughed, he just couldn't help himself. Jenna was a rare treat in this world and he loved her very much. He asked her about the vampire and if she was going to live forever.

"Not that I'm aware of. But I should make you aware of something that we've done for you. Quincey, he works for me, has for a number of years. Anyway, he has spoken to Thomas regarding you." He asked her what she meant. "Thomas has been warned, you might say. Quincey told him to back off from what he's been doing. Not that I think he will. It's been my experience that fools and idiots never change their colors, don't you think? Anyway, did you know that you aren't the first person that Thomas has done this too? Nor, do I think, you will be the last. But the bartender at the place where you met

Thomas, he's been told either straighten up or die. Simple as that."

"Quincey Anderson?" Jenna nodded. "Oh my, you do have some pretty powerful friends, don't you? And you didn't have to have him step in on my account, Jenna. I'm sure that Thomas will back off when he realizes that I'm not going to take his shit."

"Do you think? I don't. Quincey said that Thomas believes that he's killed you. I'm pretty sure that you know it was him that shot you. His plan was to kill you, then move into your home." Forrest leaned back on the sofa and tried to wrap his mind around that. "Quincey said that the man is a fool, and he will gladly take him out for you. I have it on good authority that not only will Thomas continue on as he has in the past, but that he'll not leave here as he'd been warned to do. The man is a fool."

"Yes, he is at that. And I figured he shot at me, but not that he intended to kill me. Why does he think that was the plan?" Jenna told him that he'd had a little taste of the man, then raped his small mind. "Christ. Remind me never to piss you off."

"Deal." She stood up and he started to as well. "Don't do that. I know that you're not hurt, not too badly anyway, but there is no reason for us to play this game any longer, Forrest. I think we're friends enough that we can skip the ceremony, don't you? Also, if you wouldn't mind, I would like to consider you family now. Jake is for the most part my only relative that I love and care for, and as his mate, I think of you as my grandson as well. What do you think?"

"Yes, I'd like that very much. And no, I'm not hurt too

badly. Mostly it's just a little pain, but if I can shift, I'll be as good as new." She nodded. "Jenna, what about his parents? How do you think they're going to react to finding out that we're lovers?"

She started to answer him, but paused when Jake appeared in the doorway. He was pale and a little sweaty looking as he made his way to the chair, but otherwise fine as he leaned back and closed his eyes. Forrest felt his cat move along his skin, the need to protect him was so profound, and he was surprised by that. Jake looked at him then.

"I felt that." Forrest nodded. "Will he, I don't know, shift now? I'm not sure just how all that works. I'm pretty sure that the crap I read on the Internet is just that, crap. You'll have to explain a few things to me."

"I'd be glad to. And no, he's not going to take me. He only does that when there is danger that he feels that I can't handle. But he is pretty antsy about getting me healed up. Danger could come to us at any time, and he wants things just right." Jake nodded and Forrest had to smile. "Are you afraid of him?"

"No. I haven't any idea why, but no, I'm not afraid of either of you." Forrest nodded, then Jenna cleared her throat. "Grandma, I'm sorry that you had to witness that with Dad. He's usually so discreet when he tells me what a failure I am."

"He's an ass." Jake nodded and Forrest laughed. "I had no idea that he'd become such a snob either. To hear him tell it, he's the first and only Winslow ever born. What an idiot. And that wife of his.... Jake, I just don't know how you stayed there for the first eighteen years of your life. I surely don't. I certainly didn't raise him that way. To think that he wants you to live with that monster. And after all the information I sent him about her too. You'd think that your happiness would be much more important to him than what a few of their so called friends care about." Grandma shivered, and Forrest thought he could have easily gone out and killed the man for her.

"Father has always been one to make sure that we kept up appearances. I think that is the only reason that he let me go to college to become a lawyer. Because it was a good job with status." Jake turned to Forrest as he continued talking to his grandma. "I don't think he's going to be very happy about a lot of things in the future where I'm concerned. Especially when it comes out about Forrest and me."

"Sadly, no he will not. But I'd not let it worry you overly much. You're my grandson, and that's all you should think about. All I care about is that you're going to be happy." She made her way to the door and Forrest wanted to call her back. If she left then he'd be alone with Jake, and that made him a little nervous. "I should be going now. Oh, before I forget, you have a housekeeper now. She starts tomorrow. Her name is Mary. She's a wolf, so don't let her eat your father if he should come back and piss her off. Mary is going to keep an eye on the two of you. I don't want anyone shooting my two favorite boys."

Neither of them moved when the door closed. Forrest didn't have any idea what he was supposed to do now. He'd not been alone like this with Jake since he'd met him. And even in the hospital, there had been staff just on the other side of the door.

"We could order in." Forrest nodded. "You have to say something. I can't stand the thought of what you might be thinking right now."

"I'm thinking I'm terrified out of my mind." Jake nodded. "I'd very much like to shift. I have a pounding headache, and that'll take care of any of the last of the pains I have as well."

"All right." When he stood up, so did Forrest. "I'm assuming that you'll need to be outside to make it easier on you. Like I said before, I don't know how any of this works."

"I have to be naked." Jake just stood there. "I'll go out on the deck and strip down. Then you can either wait in here or out there. I just want to run for a bit. I have a lot of nervous energy."

"I'd like to watch you, if you don't mind." Forrest said he didn't as he made his way to the deck. "Does it hurt? I mean, like a lot of pain?"

"None, as a matter of fact. I just let the cat consume me and it's fine. It does hurt when he has to do it quickly, like from man to cat in a matter of seconds. But that only happens when, as I said before, he feels that he can handle something better than I can. If you watch me do it now, you'll see that it's not as quick as some of the books make it out to be." Jake followed him out and Forrest could only stare. "Christ, this is all yours?"

The yard was massive, and well maintained. He looked at the beautiful trees that lined a garden like area at the very back of the property, to the pool that looked so inviting that he wanted to swim despite the fact that it was cold out. A pool house as well as another smaller version of the main house sat in the back too. It was nestled deep in the woods like a faerie grove, with plants and trees surrounding it.

"Yes. It's beautiful, isn't it? Carol never appreciated this part of the house and land. When I first got out of college, back when my grandda was still alive, he said that a man who had a nice degree like I had deserved a good home. He never cared for Carol, but he loved me. When she was looking for an address, the only thing that mattered to her, Grandda was finding me a home. One that I could grow old in. And land. He told me once that there wasn't anyone out making more of that, so I should have as much as I could put my hands on." Forrest asked him how much he owned. "There is just under four hundred acres here. When he bought this for me there was less than fifty. I have been buying up what I could surrounding this place. I also own a few thousand acres out west, and a couple of homes in Europe. Like I said, no one is making any more, so I wanted to keep as much as I could for myself."

"Christ, Jake. That's wonderful. And your grandfather must be laughing his ass off about now. But I'm assuming that Carol hasn't any idea how much you're really worth." He said that it never came up. "You sly devil, you. How did I not know you were so smart?"

"People underestimate me because I'm so quiet. My father included. He has it in his head that I'm struggling. But in fact, if I never worked another day in my life, I'd still have more than he ever will." Forrest laughed. "My grandma and I, we own a lot of other things too. We formed this partnership about the time I married Carol. Everything we have is in this corporation. And since Carol signed a pre-nup when we were engaged, she can't touch any of it, not even if I pass away before her."

"How much are you worth? And so you know, I come from money too. My mother's parents left me a nice nest egg, as they called it. This was, of course, before anyone knew I was gay. But I've been able to invest wisely and to get a nice return on some stocks that I have." Jake told him how much he was worth. Forrest could only stare. "Are you fucking me? Forty billion? As in billions?"

"Yes. I told you, I've done well." He was embarrassed. Jake's face was red and getting hotter as they stood there. He could almost smell it. "You should shift now. I'd very much like to see your cat. Please?"

He was stalling. Forrest wanted to ask him what firms he invested in. How much of a return did he have, and if he would help him. Forrest's money, all three million of it, seemed like a drop in the bucket alongside of Jake's. But he was right, it was well past time for him to show him his other half.

Taking off his shirt, he opted to leave his pants on. They were the kind that would tear away if he didn't remove them, and he thought for now it might be easier to shift with them on. Forrest wasn't sure why, but he thought that if he were naked right now, here on the deck where no one could see them, that he'd never shift. He wanted his mate right now.

CHAPTER 7

Carol let the phone ring and ring. Her daddy was pissed at her. Mother was having a fit because of the mess on the front lawn, and the staff wasn't giving her anything that she demanded. What were servants for, she thought, if not to abuse and take advantage of? Carol didn't understand why the moving company hadn't done as she wanted and left it all on Jake's grass, but here it was. All seventy-four pieces of it, set up like it was sitting in her house right there on the front lawn. She wanted to murder someone, and if someone didn't answer the phone soon, it was going to be the stupid moving company owner. She picked up the chips she'd stolen from the pantry an hour ago when she couldn't get anyone to make her a sandwich.

"Harvard Moving. How may I help you?" Carol had to chew faster when the woman finally answered the phone. "Hello? This is Harvard Moving."

"This is Carol Winslow. I have a complaint about how I was treated today." The woman said that the conversation was being recorded. That was the second time this week that she'd heard that. Why on earth did anyone want to have a recording of her? "I had your company move my things to my house. Yet here it is, on my parents' lawn and not where I wanted it."

"You said this is Carol Winslow?" Carol said it was. "Mrs. Winslow, Mr. Winslow refused the shipment. The driver said he spoke to Mr. Winslow and he said that the two of you are no longer living together, and that we should take the furniture back to the storage units. And since they were already rented again, there was nowhere for us to go but to the address on the slip. I'm not sure what else you expected us to do when you never answered the calls we placed to you."

"My cell phone is temporally out of service. That's something else I'm taking care of." The woman on the other end said nothing. "Look, I need for you to come here and do something with my things. My dad is having a fit and it's supposed to rain tonight. I can't have my things ruined because your company didn't do what I told them to do. I'll expect you here within the hour since I've been trying to reach you all afternoon."

"We're a business with a great many other customers that aren't as demanding as you. And if you mean deliver furniture to a house that you no longer reside at, that's not going to happen either." Carol said that it was her home. "I don't think so. Nor do I think the person living there thinks so. Mr. Winslow was very clear on the fact that you don't have any rights to the house."

"My husband is delusional. He thinks that just because I

took everything out of my house that he has the right to divorce me. Well, I've told him that he's not going to do that and we're working out the details. But until then I want you to take my things to your place; I'm sure that you have room for it somewhere. Even if you have to leave it on the trucks until I call you. Just, I don't want it to be damaged. Jake has to get his head out of his ass over this, and its taking longer than I thought it would." The woman said nothing. "Are you listening to me, you stupid woman? I said to come and get my things off the front lawn before my daddy gets madder. You don't want to see him angry."

"I'm sure that I don't. And if you call me stupid again, this conversation is finished." Carol pulled the phone from her ear and stared at it. No one spoke to her this way, and she wanted to scream at her to have respect. Her husband was a fucking attorney and could own her ass. "Now, this is what is going to happen. I am not going to send my men out there to get your things off the lawn, and even if they were to go out there, we'd not be storing it in any of our containers. In your agreement with this firm, you were told that once you vacated a storage locker that you gave up all rights to it, as you were a day to day rental. And once you had us take the things out we were obligated to put it somewhere. It was out of our hands when Mr. Winslow showed us proof that you no longer have any rights to the house or its property. So in turn, as we have no place to store your things, it's been returned, in full, to the address you used on the paperwork. I think, now that I've spoken to you, that I understand why they took such pleasure in placing your things the way that they did. You aren't a very pleasant person, are you?"

"Now you listen here, bitch. You get out here now and get my things put away. I don't want to have to call my husband on you. He's a great attorney." The woman said ex-husband, like she enjoyed saying it. "He's not going to be my ex-husband, damn it. I will say when and if he can leave me. And when he does, it'll be because he's dead, not thinking of leaving me without my house."

"I guess you're going to have to learn to stop calling yourself Mrs. anything and move on then." The line went dead, the long tone of it making her want to throw the thing across the room.

Before she could act on that however, it was jerked from her hand and set gently in the cradle. Carol thought that made her twice as angry, that someone could be so calm while she was hot with it. As she stood up to tear into her mother, she told her to shut up.

"I've called in a favor and the things will be picked up in an hour." Carol didn't even thank her. Her mom wasn't doing this for her but because of the neighbors, no doubt. "I've called Jake's attorney and let him know that your father is making a large donation to the local charity. It'll be a nice—"

"What kind of donation? If he has any money to be donating to someone, he should give it to me. I can do a lot of shopping with that sort of cash." Her mother told her to hush. "I will not hush. What did he donate?"

"The things on the lawn, of course. I was afraid that if it got rained on, no one would want it. As it is now, I'm not sure who in their right mind would. Carol, you've got to have the worst taste in style of anyone I've ever met." Carol could only stare at her. She'd called a charity to come for her beautiful things? How could she? "Also, you'll love this too, Jake has sent someone for his car. He said that since you and he will be divorced soon that he's not going to make payments on the insurance. I'm assuming you know that he's cut your phone off."

"My car? How can he take my car? That's fucking mine. Mother, why are you doing this to me?" She asked her what she meant. "Jake? You? Daddy? What is wrong with you people? Have you no idea how much…? If one piece of my things are touched by some charity person, I will murder you. I swear to Christ, I'm going to find a gun and kill you with it."

"Which brings me to another thing. Your father and I talked it over, and you have until the end of the week to get out of our home. It's going to be hard enough on us when your father gets his lawyers in on this, but in the long run, we've decided that it's better than having you here all the time. Think of that. Money has taken a second seat to having our daughter around. Anyway, you're disruptive to the staff, rude to the drivers, and you are driving us nuts with your whining all the time. We've decided, happily by the way, that you made your bed and now you have to lie in it. But not in our home." Her mom moved around the room and tossed things in the trash that she found to her distaste. "You're such a pig, Carol, and I don't care for the way you act as if this is yours to treat as you wish."

"You told the servants not to bother with my room. What did you expect to happen, Mother? That this room would clean itself?" She sat down on the edge of the unmade bed. "Jake took the servants away from me as well. But he never said a word when he had to clean up after me. I don't know why you think

121

you can. You have staff here; I'm only making them work for their checks."

"You would say that, Carol. I can say whatever I want because you're here invading my home." Her mother had no idea what she was talking about, and Carol was simply too exhausted to explain it to her. "You have to find yourself a place to live. We'll help you out for the first month with money, but after — "

"Give me the money now and I'll leave the room so you can make the servants come in here and clean up. That way I can have my hair done, and my nails. They're chipped, and I feel so horrible about the way I've looked lately." Carol put out her hand, waiting for the cash that she knew her mother had on her person. "Well? I have things to do today. Jake isn't doing what I want and I have to go see him. I need to look my best."

"I'm not giving you money, Carol. That ship sailed a long time ago. You'll have help in the form of us paying the first month's rent and the deposit. After that, I'm afraid you'll have to find yourself a job. I doubt very much that Jake will pay you any alimony." Carol stood up and her mom backed away. "When did you become such a horrible person, Carol? We didn't raise you to be like this."

"Jake is not going to divorce me. He's just not. And I would very much appreciate it if everyone would quit saying that to me. He doesn't have my permission to do anything that I don't want. Give me the money, Mother. I kid you not when I tell you that I've had about enough of this kicking me around shit." She moved to her mom, glad to see the fear there. "You're also going to replace my things that you donated without my permission. I will not have you treating me and my pretty things like they're nothing."

"Get out of my house." Before she could think that she shouldn't lash out, Carol hit her mom. When she staggered back, almost falling, Carol decided that she wanted to see that, her mom hurt. "Carol, I'm calling the police."

Leaping at her, Carol knew that she was going to be in trouble for this. Her daddy would have to pay someone to clean up yet another of her messes. As her fists pounded into her mother, all Carol could think about was revenge. And that no one would tell her that Jake was stupid enough to divorce her again.

Falling back from her mom, she sat there. It occurred to her that she'd have to shower again now, and redo her make-up and hair. Her mother had ruined another thing for her. Carol had really liked the outfit she'd put on today. Standing up, she started for the shower and remembered the cash. It took ten minutes of searching her mother to realize that she really hadn't had any money, and was pissed all over again.

"I won't hit you this time, but you will learn to not do things to piss me off again." As she stripped off her ruined things she made her way to the bathroom again. Damn it, she was going to have to scrub herself hard to get the stains off her.

After getting refreshed, she pulled on a skirt that she didn't care for and blamed her mother for that as well. She'd driven her to this; it was her own fault for being such a horrible bitch. Leaving her room and the door open, hoping someone would go in and clean up her things, Carol made her way out of the house and to the cars in the drive. Hers, of course, was missing.

"Fuckers." Going to the garage angered her more. There were several cars in the place, most of them cleaner than her room had ever been. But there were no keys, at least none that she could get to. For some reason—and she was going to have to talk to him about that—her daddy had them locked up. She'd have to walk, she supposed, and that wasn't going to make her day any better. Then she spotted her mother's car. As much as she hated that thing, her mother had left the keys in it so she took it. "Someone is going to have to get their shit in gear around here. Or I'll be bashing in a few more heads."

~~~

Forrest stretched his body out, feeling better than he had in a very long time. He was nervous; being shot would do that to a person, he supposed. But he felt good at this moment. As he and his cat made it around the large wooded area, all he could think about was Jake, and what he might be doing right now. When a twig snapped behind him, he turned quickly, only to find that Jake had followed him.

"You're really fast as a cat. I guess it would be because of the four feet." Reaching out to speak to him, not sure that he could, Forrest touched his mind. "I can feel you there. Like a thought or something."

That's just what it is. You can speak to me this way as well. Jake nodded. Forrest had a feeling that he wasn't really paying attention. *Tell me what it is. I'd very much like to know.*

"You're going to think I'm nuts. Or at the very least, a bastard." Forrest laughed. "Okay, I want you to move in here with me on a permanent basis. If the offer still holds, I'd very much like to be your partner in your firm as well. Actually, in all things."

You know what you're saying, don't you? We'll be ridiculed. What your father said, it will be much worse. I have a feeling that he's going to make it that way for us. He nodded. *Jake, we can move on this slowly.*

"I don't think I want to. I've been thinking a great deal about my life. Not just with Carol, but before that. Long before I married or even went to college. I think that I've always been a homosexual." Forrest laid down when Jake sat on a nearby stump. "In high school, even in middle school, I never much cared for women. Not to say that I didn't admire them, I did. But not for sex, or even for conversation. They were just boring, I thought. Talking about their hair, what they had for dinner. It was like talking to a wall sometimes, one that was covered in mirrors."

Boring, or did you think you were better than them? Jake asked him what he meant. *You came from money. Had a great deal of it. Was the fact that you didn't want to marry beneath you a part of it, or something more?*

"You're a snob." They both laughed. "No, not that. Though I think my parents thought that I should have been. No, it was more that I found the boys that I saw more attractive. They were prettier. I liked the way their clothing fit them, shirts molded to their frames. You must think that I'm nuts."

No, go on. Tell me why you think this. I mean, you have come to this relationship with me very easily, I think. Not much in the way of denial. There was no second guessing things. Tell me why you think this.

"Exactly that. I mean, being in love with you, it was as

125

natural for me as breathing. I didn't have to think about if you were going to make me happy, if you were going to be there for me. I just knew that you would be." Forrest asked him if he did love him. "Yes. And I'm happy to say that you're the only person for me. I've never felt this way for anyone before."

Forrest was stuck on the fact that he loved him. Jake Winslow loved him. When Jake got up to pace, his body stiff with whatever he was thinking, Forrest decided that now would be a good time to come out to him as well.

The first time I realized that I wasn't like the other kids in my class, I was twelve. It might have been a bit before that, but I knew then, when Sally Ramshaw showed me her breasts. It was.... All I could think about at the time was, it wasn't what I had thought it would be. And it wasn't all that sexy. Jake asked him if he thought all twelve-year-old girls had sexy breasts. *I don't know, but Sally had some big ones. She developed long before the other girls in class had. Anyway, she asked me to touch her. Just her breasts. It was like touching a piece of that dough stuff that comes in colors that kids play with.*

"Wow, that's a pretty gross way to put it. I'm hoping you didn't tell her that." He said that he'd not. "I'm assuming that after that, you went out to touch more breasts."

Well, I had to be sure, didn't I? They were still laughing as Jake sat again. *By the time I was fourteen, I was finding my way around the sexual aspects of others. Men mostly, who wanted little boys to give them a thrill. I'm not proud of what I did, but it did make me aware that I wasn't into boobs or girls.*

"There was a study group that I joined. I couldn't do much in the way of getting any work done at home, so I'd find study partners that I could work with. Carol would want me to take her places, see the things that she purchased that day. Mostly being a pain in the ass. Anyway, I joined this group of men about my age." Jake looked off into the trees and Forrest waited. He had a feeling that Jake needed to say this more than he wanted him to hear it. "Bill, that was his name, he was sitting next to me in the big library one night when he brushed his leg against mine. It was innocent enough, I guess. Or I thought so until lately. But when I didn't pull away, he put his hand on my thigh."

Forrest could see all the emotions on Jake's face. Embarrassment. Excitement. There was even a little shyness there, just enough that Forrest knew that he was still trying to deal with what the two of them were doing.

"After we finished studying, I headed to the bathroom. I was as hard as stone and confused. But he followed me in there." Jake said nothing, and Forrest thought it best if he just waited. He really wanted to ask him what had happened. If he'd been all right, but Jake needed to tell it in his own words. "He didn't rush me. Or for that matter touch me. But he stood there, staring at me. Then, just as I was ready to leave, he rubbed his hand over his cock. He was…he was really hard too."

As Forrest sat there, not saying anything, all sorts of things went through his mind. Rape, which he dismissed almost immediately. He didn't seem afraid, just really confused. Blackmail? Also not likely. Forrest thought he would have taken care of that immediately. Or Jenna would have.

"He took his pants down. His cock was hard and leaking at the tip, and all I could think about was tasting what was there. Freeing my own seemed the most natural thing to do. And as we stood there, each of us holding our cocks, I felt free." Jake got up to pace again, walking back and forth gently, as if he was lightening up with each word he said. "When he came I did as well. My balls ached, they'd been so full, and when his cum touched me, just on my belly, I came a second time."

Did he say anything to you? Touch you in any way afterwards? Jake said no, it hadn't been like that. *What was it like?*

"I'm not sure. A mutual understanding that this was a one-time thing? That we were just getting off because we needed it? I don't know. But it was as if we understood each other on another level." He laughed a little. "The next time I saw him, he ignored me. I did the same to him. It was as if we had agreed that it hadn't happened. But you know what? I was sort of sad about that as well. Like I'd been left out of something."

He turned around then. Forrest thought he looked sad or just lonely, both emotions that he knew so well. And when he pulled his shirt up and over his head, Forrest stood up as well.

The shift from cat to man was quick. He stood there, naked, and thought of what they were about to embark on here. Not like in the hospital. That had been born of desperation, of a need that had nothing to do with sex and more to do with just the necessity to be held. At least that was what he'd felt. But now... now, here with Jake in the darkening woods, both of them on the same page, Forrest felt as if this was going to be their first time.

Jake kicked off his shoes, toeing them off as he held onto the tree behind him. Forrest could see his cock was thick; even through his open pants. Stepping closer, just enough to touch, Jake moaned.

"I've thought of nothing else but having you touch me. Tasting your skin. Feeling your heart beating under my fingers." Forrest touched Jake's throat, ran his fingers down his chest to his muscled belly. "I need to taste you, Jake. Will you let me?"

"Yes. Oh yes, please."

Forrest dropped to his knees in front of Jake. His body smelled delicious, his skin dewy from need. Licking a path from his navel to his hip, he thought his need was almost equal to his own.

Nipping at his skin, Forrest had to make himself slow down, to take his time at this. He also wanted it to be perfect. When Jake curled his fingers through his hair, he looked up at him and nearly came then.

Raw emotion. Love and happiness. Need and desire. Forrest laid his head on his belly and watched him as he slid his hand up his thigh to his balls. Holding them, rolling gently, all he could think about was that Jake was his.

Taking him into his mouth was heaven. Jake was thicker than he was, but not as long. When he swallowed him past the back of his throat, he heard him moan again, his breath catch. Encouraged now, Forrest rolled his tongue around the curve of his cock, along the length of him when he pulled free. The more he tasted of him, the more that he wanted.

"Suck me."

He did as commanded, moving up and down over his shaft quickly. Jake rode his mouth, hard pounding strokes that had Forrest holding his hips so he'd not come unseated. His own cock was heavy with the need to release.

Sliding his fingers along Jake's ass, he touched his fingers to his tight hole. Jake paused but didn't stop him when Forrest pushed forward, just enough to feel his heat. And when he slid past the tight muscles there, Jake screamed.

His cum filled Forrest's mouth, slid down his chin to his chest as he pounded him. Forrest grabbed his own cock, fisting himself. When Jake cried out again, screaming out his name, Forrest pulled back, let the hot cream of him spray over his face and chest.

Jake moved back, falling against the tree as Forrest stood up. When he turned, telling him to hold on, Jake moved up behind him. Closing his eyes, waiting for the pleasure pain, he cried out when Jake entered him, filled him with his cock as he stood there.

"Fuck me. Hard." He wasn't sure that he was going to; his body seemed stiff as he held him. "Jake, I need this. Please."

It was slow at first; Jake was taking him gently enough that he knew he was holding back. But then, like a switch had been flipped, he began to fuck him, his cock pistoning in and out as his balls touched his own. Forrest wrapped his hand around his cock again, needing to come when Jake did. But almost as soon as he touched himself, Jake reached around him, wrapping his hot hands around him and moved up and down his shaft in rhythm to his fucking.

He was in heaven and the burning pits of hell at the same time. He wanted to come but also needed to make it last. Then he felt it, felt the exact moment that Jake came, and he cried out with it. Heat filled him. His cat cried out, screaming along his skin as he was marked as well. And just as he was thinking it was enough, just to have Jake be satisfied, his own climax roared over him and took him under when Jake bit hard into his shoulder.

CHAPTER 8

Jake was giddy one moment and terrified out of his mind the next. He looked over at the man, a man sleeping next to him, and wondered how he'd been so lucky. Smiling, he got up from the bed and made his way to his office. He was too happy to sleep right now.

Forrest had passed out. Jake had thought that he'd killed him. He knew that was just crazy, people didn't really die from fantastic sex, but it had made him feel like he'd won the bronze, silver, and gold in sex. As he turned on his monitor, he thought of the things that they'd talked about on the way back to the house.

"We'll have to take it easy." Jake asked Forrest why. When he laughed, Jake did as well. "What I meant was, we'll have to move you into this sort of sex slowly. I might be painful for you."

"Oh." He had an idea it was going to be very painful, but

didn't care. "I've been reading up on it. Also watching videos again. There are a lot of things out there that aren't so.... Well, like we had, beautiful."

"Yes. I've seen some really nasty stuff. And heard worse." Forrest took his hand in his as they continued. "If you need answers to the million and one questions I'm sure you have, you can ask me about them. I'm sure that together, we can figure things out. A way that is mutually pleasurable for us both."

After getting back to the house, they'd gone to bed. Exhaustion took them both under; Jake was out in seconds, and he was sure that Forrest had been as well. It was nice, he thought, just to know that he was not only happy, but in love too. Jake sat at his desk and turned on his computer with a sappy smile on his face.

Pulling up his email account, he saw that there were four from Carol's father and one from Carol. He pulled out his phone to see if he'd missed something, and saw that he had fifty-three missed calls as well as messages. Pulling up the first message, he opened the first email that he'd been sent and read it as the service went through what he needed to do to hear the messages. Tyler's voice was the first one that came up.

"There's been a terrible accident." Then he sobbed. "Belinda is in the hospital on life support. I don't know what all has happened but.... Can you call me? I know that we've not been on the best of terms, but I really would like to speak to you."

The second message was a repeat of the first, Tyler asking him to call no matter the time. He also explained a little more, saying that he thought that Carol had hurt her mother and he didn't know what to do.

Dialing the number that he'd left him, Jake wondered if he'd been correct, that Carol had really hurt her mom bad enough to have her put on life support. By the time the phone had rang three times, Jake was sure he'd misheard him. When Tyler answered, Jake simply said his name and it opened a storm of sobs from the poor man.

"She's not doing well. They said that she has brain damage. How could she do this to her own mother? We'd talked, Belinda and me, and we decided after the furniture fiasco that we couldn't have her there much longer. She was rude, Jake. To everyone. I'm so sorry. We made so many mistakes with Carol. And involved you in them." He cried harder; Jake's heart was breaking for the older man. "When I got the call, my first thought was that someone broke in, robbed us, you know? Then I came here with the butler, and Williams told me that Carol had left behind her bloodied clothing after doing it."

"What have the police said, or have you called them?" Tyler said he'd called them first thing after getting there. "Do you know where she is now? Carol, I mean, have you heard from her?"

"No. Not even to tell me that she's sorry. I have no idea, Jake, not one clue as to what would make her snap like that. Not that it takes all that much. She's not right, I'm sure you already figured that out." Jake didn't want to tell him that he thought Carol was more than a little off, but he seemed to understand. "I was surprised, if you want to know the truth, that you finally kicked her out. Upset at first too. You have no idea how much this has cost me and my wife. So much. I would have thought.... Well, she wasn't easy to live with as a child, and only got worse

135

as she grew older. I swear, Jake, I had no idea how bad she'd gotten. Like she should have it all just because she thinks she should. I'm so sorry."

"I'm all right now. I'm very glad to know that you're not mad at me for this. She did this on her own, but I think it was long in coming, as you said." Jake looked up when he heard someone clear their throat. It was Forrest. "I'm going to come in there to sit with you. You shouldn't be doing this alone."

"Would you?" He told Forrest briefly what was going on. "You have company? I'm so sorry, Jake. I shouldn't have called whining to you. I just…I really don't know why I called you. But as soon as I found out, you were the first person that I thought of. I need to talk to you too. Tell you some things you might not be aware of. It's time…well, past time to get this thing out in the open."

"I'm not sure this is the time, Tyler, but we'll be in. Forrest Stout and I, we'll be there in an hour. And you didn't whine, you're a man that has been hurt by his child." As soon as he made arrangements to go by Tyler's house and pick up a few things for him that the butler would have ready, he told Forrest what was going on.

"She's off the reservation, you know that, don't you?" Jake nodded. "Tyler called you; did he say why?"

"No. Only that he thought of me when he figured out that Carol had done it. I knew she was a little off, but to hurt someone like it sounds like she did is really something I never expected of her. He also mentioned that he had things to tell me. Things to get out in the open. I have no idea what he might mean by that. Did you find anything?" Forrest sat down as he shook his head, and that was when he noticed that he was dressed. "Were you leaving?"

"No. I mean, yes, with you." Forrest leaned back on the couch. "You should understand something. I should have said something before, but I can feel your emotions, and if I need to, I can touch your mind and see what's going on. All I knew was you were hurting and I wanted to know why. I hope that's all right."

"Yes. It's fine. I just...I guess you might say that I'm still insecure about this, about us." Forrest said he was too. "That's good to know."

Jake got dressed and they made their way to the hospital. It wasn't a long trip, but it was a little nerve wracking. Carol had nearly killed her mother. What sort of person did something like that?

Just as they were pulling into the parking lot, Forrest asked him if he thought he should just wait for him to come back.

"Wait? You mean out here? Why would you think that?" Forrest only shrugged. "Are you afraid that he'll, I don't know, figure things out? I don't care if he does or not. I didn't do anything wrong."

"No, but it could be hard on you later. I'm just saying if you want to play this low key, I understand." Jake said he wasn't sure what he wanted but got out of the car. "Jake, people are going to talk."

"I know that. You think I don't know that? But right now, I don't care. I might in an hour or never, but right now, I'm happy being with you and that's how I'm going to play it. If that's not what you want, I think you should tell me." Forrest

137

smiled, a huge grin that seemed to take up most of his face. "What?"

"You have come a long way, grasshopper." Jake was still laughing when they entered the hospital with the suitcase they'd gotten from the Lane residence. "I think I like this more assertive you. You're kind of scary and sexy at the same time."

"Don't get used to it. I'm all spongey on the inside." He was too. Malleable and scared, happy and ready to take on the world, all at the same time. "I have no idea if I will ever be assertive, as you said, but I do feel better about myself. And where I am in my life."

Tyler was sitting in the hall when they arrived on the floor. He looked beaten and exhausted. As soon as he saw them, Tyler got up and hugged them both, crying about how much he appreciated them coming in. Forrest said he'd go get them something to eat and some coffee. When he was gone Jake sat next to the elderly man.

"The doctor just came by. He wants to talk to me. I asked him to wait until you were here." Jake said that was fine, he'd be there for him. "Thank you. As I said before, I know that we didn't see eye to eye on things, but I'm certainly glad you came in. But I really have something to tell you. Something that I fully regret now."

"Its fine, Tyler, really. I'm glad that I could be here for you. You are my father-in-law regardless of the other things going on." He nodded but said nothing. "Have you had any more information from the police?"

"No. I mean sort of indirectly. My attorney is keeping tabs on things. Telling me what they find out and what they're doing.

Carol was last seen at the mall, trying her best to get someone to let her use your credit cards to buy herself some clothing." Jake told him he'd heard from one of the stores earlier and had forgotten about it. "She's a monster."

"She was never violent like that when we were together. I mean, she has a hell of a temper, but she's never hurt me." Tyler pulled a file out of a briefcase and held it. "Tyler, they'll find her. She'll get some help and it'll be all right."

"I want you to read this. Tonight if you can. It's about Carol, and just one of the few things that we did to keep her out of prison or worse. When she was sixteen she killed a man and his wife. They were in front of her at the movie theater, just waiting in line like the rest of the people. But they bought the last tickets for this movie that she wanted to see." He handed him the file. "Carol told them to give her one of their tickets. She explained to them, in a calm voice I'm told, that she wanted to see it and that they both didn't need to go in at the same time. That if they didn't hand over one of the tickets she was going to hurt them. The man, he told her that he and his wife had been saving for this event for weeks and that Carol wasn't getting their tickets. Then he turned his back on her."

Jake opened the file. He nearly closed it again when he saw the pictures. They were in color glossy eight by tens. Jake turned to the second photo of the crime scene, and then looked up at Tyler when he continued.

"She broke his neck. Just jumped up on his back and twisted his head until it snapped. Do you have any idea how much strength it takes to do that?" Jake said he thought it would take a lot. "Yes. To break a person's neck fatally it would take the

139

equivalent of a person hitting a windshield while not wearing a seat belt. And an upper body strength to turn the head with enough force to just snap it."

"And you're sure that she did it?" Jake was told to go to the next picture. "Christ, Tyler. I had no idea."

Carol was on the back of the man in the first photo, her hands wrapped around his head in a way that he'd seen on television. He looked up at Tyler, asking him about the woman. He looked away before staring at him.

"She was four months pregnant. Carol hit her so many times in the face that she was only identified by the tattoo that was on her ankle. There wasn't much of her head left. Carol had used a brick, one that had been just laying there when she'd gone into her rage." Tyler leaned back, his body spent. "Then she took the ticket from the woman's dead husband's hand and proceeded into the theater. As if nothing had happened. Those pictures, they're from a camera that some shop had outside because of a robbery. Otherwise, we might never have known the extent of her violence that night."

"What did you do, Tyler? I'm sure you had this covered up. How did you make that happen?" He cried again, telling Jake how sorry he was. That he shouldn't have done anything, but she was his child. "What did you do?"

"I paid them. All of them. Millions of dollars to keep her out of prison. I should have just let her go, let her get the help she needed." Tyler looked at him again. "Then she met you and I thought.... Well, I had hoped that you could fix her for me."

~~~

Forrest reached out to Jake again. There wasn't any

connection. It was as if he was walking into a wall every time he tried to contact him. Driving around town didn't help Forrest find him either. He was turning down the main street near the hospital when he thought he saw him walking. Parking the car, he got out and nearly sobbed with relief when he found him sitting on a park bench near the river.

"Jake? Jake, are you all right?" Nothing, not even an acknowledgement that he'd spoken to him. Touching his fingers to his arm had him turning, but still no words left his mouth. "Jake, I've been looking for you."

"He wanted me to fix her." He nodded, not entirely sure what Jake was talking about. "He knew what sort of person she was long before I met her. He knew this, Forrest, and let her marry me."

"I didn't talk to Tyler, Jake. I don't know what happened. I came back with coffee and sandwiches and you were both gone. The nurse said you'd walked away and Tyler went to see his wife." Jake nodded and stood. "Tell me what's going on. Your mind is a jumble of thoughts right now."

"Carol. She really is a monster." Forrest walked with him, not interrupting him, hoping to get an idea what was going on. "She killed a couple for a movie ticket several years ago. I have the file. Or I did have it."

"The one on the chair where you were sitting at the hospital?" Jake nodded. "I have it. I saw the pictures and didn't want to leave that on the.... Are you saying that Carol did that? Killed those people?"

"Yes. And their unborn child too." Forrest stopped walking, his head trying hard to wrap around what Jake had just said.

141

When he caught up with him, Jake was still talking. "...looked it up and it said that it would take a grown man with a weight of about two-fifty to do something like that. But there she was, leaping on his back and turning his head like he was nothing more than a twig. Then she bludgeoned the wife to death."

Jake stopped moving, and Forrest nearly ran into him when he turned around. He looked terrified, like he was fearful that Carol would do the same to him. Forrest said his name again and was glad when he started walking back the way they'd come.

Jake didn't speak during the rest of the walk. Nor did he talk on the way home. When the car stopped, Jake got out and walked to the house and went inside. Forrest pulled out his cell phone and called his friend at the morgue. He asked him about the murders.

"I remember that. A younger couple, not even in their mid-twenties I think." He asked what he knew. "Nothing much. The bodies came in one night while I was just leaving work, and before I came to work two days later, they were gone and no one was talking about it. And no matter who I asked no one spoke about it."

Pay off. Forrest knew that it happened more often than not with the rich and stupid. He even had a name for it. Bloody cash. He'd never actually known anyone that had had it done to them, nor a family that had been paid off. But a lawyer didn't get far in this business without encountering it at least once.

He asked his buddy to see if he could dig anything up. It had been about fourteen years, so maybe enough time had gone by to get someone to loosen up a little. As he made his way into the house, he wasn't surprised to find Jake sitting in the dark living room holding a glass of some sort of amber liquid in one hand and the house phone in the other. Taking the phone from him, Forrest put it on the cradle. He sat across from him and waited. He didn't have to wait long.

"Tyler killed himself about an hour ago. First he killed Belinda, then himself. He left a note, telling the world that he could no longer live with himself and that he had disowned his daughter. That was all, just that." Forrest asked him if he was all right. "I'm not sure, really. I never cared for Tyler; Belinda was all right, nice to me when I'd go to events at their home, but I didn't know her well. The doctor told the police that he'd just informed Mr. Lane that Belinda had no brain activity, nor was there going to be any quality of life for her other than in a nursing home hooked up to machines for the rest of her days."

"I'm sorry, Jake." He nodded. "What are you going to do now? I'm sure that there will be questions for you. And then there is the added fact that Carol is still out there."

"The police are searching, but I'm betting that she'll just turn up somewhere and wonder what all the fuss is about." Forrest had to agree with that. "I'm going to help them find her."

"All right." Jake looked at him, surprise written all over his face. "Did you expect me to tell you no? Or maybe tell you to leave it to the police? I don't think they're going to have any luck. She, however, thinks you and her are still going to work this out. You could lure her out faster than most, I think. But I would ask that you have the cops here or wherever."

"Yes. That's what I'm thinking as well. I just want this

over with, so we can move on." Forrest told him that's what he wanted as well. "She's going to be dangerous. I mean, more than just what she did to her mom, she's going to be coming here with one thought in her head; that I'm going to do as she tells me."

"No, you're well past that." Jake nodded and handed him the file that had been in the car. "When Tyler told you what he'd done, did he mention who had taken the case? Who had worked out the settlement?"

"My father." Forrest dropped the file and swallowed twice as he waited for the punchline. "My dad used to be this great attorney. I think that's the reason that I was allowed to become one too. To see if I could be better than him. Anyway, I did some digging and Tyler has been paying my dad ten grand every two weeks for the last fourteen years. And there was a big settlement put into his account on the day that Carol and I married."

"Your father knew." Jake said that was his assumption. "So these two couples, they get together and sort of throw you to the wolves. Christ, and I thought my family was bad. What are you going to do?"

"Tell Grandma." Forrest felt his cat shiver over him, a fear so profound that Forrest was sure his cat would never have come out for any reason now. "She'll need to know anyway, but I think this will be just what all parties deserve."

"Yeah. She's going to shit a brick. And I'm pretty sure that she's going to hit your dad with it." Jake laughed. "Have you told her yet? If you don't mind, I'd really like to be there for that. I might even take pictures."

144

"Good. Because we're having dinner here with them tomorrow night with Grandma." Jake stood up, pulled him to his body, and kissed him. When he let go, Forrest staggered slightly. "We're also going to tell them about us. So gear up."

Forrest was still standing there when he heard the front door shut. He had an idea where Jake was going and why, but he wasn't sure how to help him. Thinking of the dinner party and what it might entail, he thought of telling his parents that he was his lover. Forrest was laughing as he entered the kitchen to talk to their cook, Mary.

"We're having a party of sorts." Mary asked who was coming and when. "I'm not sure of their names, to be honest. Jake's parents and Jenna. There might be an attorney or two here, just for the fun of it, but you should also know that it's not going to be a welcoming party. More of a coming to meet the devil sort of thing, as my grandmother used to say."

"Ah. Well, we should have something that cannot be thrown at one another." Forrest said that might be good. "And a good fattening dessert. I don't believe many will enjoy that part of the meal, being that they'll be upset and leave early. But I can do that."

Forrest told her to make and do what she needed, including hiring someone to help her out with serving. He was nearly to the door again, having to get busy moving out of his rental, when Mary stopped him.

"Sir, if this is a celebration of your life with Mr. Jake, then I would suggest you invite your father as well. It might be an enlightening sort of thing to get everything out in the open." Forrest said that might be too much. "It might, but you won't

145

have to do it again, ever, if you play this correctly."

Forrest wasn't sure what he'd have to do to make his father come. The man hadn't said a word to him in over a decade. But then he thought of Jenna. The woman was going to hate him for this, but he'd ask her to do it under the guise that he wanted him to meet Jake.

Which was true, he did, but there were other things too. He wanted his dad to see how happy he was, how he'd found his mate, despite all those years of his father telling him he'd never do it. Yes, Forrest thought, this could be just the thing to do.

As he made his way to his house, he was smiling. At one point he whistled. Forrest hadn't whistled in years. And found that he liked it.

CHAPTER 9

Carol stomped to where she'd parked her mother's car. These people, she thought, were going to pay for treating her like this. And as soon as she and Jake were back together, she was going to have a party to end all parties. No matter what Jake said about it.

"He's going to have to toe the line for a bit now to get me back in his good graces. I'm not going to have him think he can do this to me again. I might not ever fully trust him again, the bastard." Carol sat in the car and laid her head on the steering wheel. "Why are people so mean to me?"

She wasn't going to cry. Not over this. Lifting her head, she stared out the window to see couples with brats going into the mall. Carol hated children of all kinds. Not just kids, but anything small and needy. They were nothing but parasites for the most part, dirty, nasty, ankle biting parasites.

Carol had known this woman once who had three of the

little buggers, all of them just as evil as the next. And when she'd been asked to hold one of them, a screaming thing, she told the woman to go fuck herself. There wasn't any way she was going to touch it.

"It's just a baby, Carol. You might want to have one of your own someday. I'm sure that Jake would be a great dad." Carol just shook her head. "Come on. I need to change the other two and you'd be helping me out."

"Drown it. Hell, drown them all." The woman looked shocked, so Carol thought she'd make sure she understood. "Seriously, you should wrap them in a trash bag and toss them in the river. It's not like anyone would miss them. Everyone knows what a horrible drain they are on you and your family. It's what I'd do if I found I'd waited too long to have it taken out of me. Christ, just get rid of them."

Being asked to leave the house hadn't been that big of a deal. Carol didn't care much for the company of other women anyway. And she'd always known that they were well beneath her in status as well as beauty. Carol could have been a contender, if not the winner, of any beauty contest she'd entered. Everyone knew that; that's what made them hate her. She looked over at the mall.

No one wanted to sell her anything. And every time she told them her name, even the lowliest of clerks, they just told her that without money or credit cards, they couldn't help her. Jake was going to have to work very hard in suing everyone that had been rotten to her this week. Starting with that little shit that ran the hair shop she'd been in just now.

"The only person in the world I thought I could talk to, and

148

he turns me down for the all mighty money." Carol wanted to go in there and teach him a lesson, as she had her mother, but the security team, the fat little fuckers, had told her to get out. "Why couldn't he have just fixed my hair for me? Why? Why? Why?"

Starting the car, she noticed that two police cruisers were entering the lot. They had their lights on and the sirens blasting as they flew past her. She knew that someone had said they were calling the police. Why would anyone care if she had messed up the place a little? It wasn't like Jake couldn't fix it for her. Or her daddy.

She thought about her mother and wondered if she'd been taken care of as yet. Carol thought she probably should have told someone that she was in her room, but she had left her door open. Christ, her mother was a pain in the ass most of the time. And if she died, well, Carol would be better off not having to listen to her harp all the time. Carol did regret that she didn't lay something down first to take care of the mess. She only hoped that there was a good carpet cleaner in the house somewhere. Besides, her daddy would be better off without her mother anyway.

Carol decided it was well past time to talk to Jake. He was going to have to give her a key sooner or later, and while the carpet and mess were being cleaned up at her parents' house, she could simply move back to her home. And while she was out and about, she could go ahead and get new things. The place, she knew, was going to need her touch after Jake living there all this time alone.

"He's probably just been living on that ugly couch and

eating out all the time. He never could do a thing without me."
Well, that wasn't entirely true. He could do a lot more around
the house than she could. "I cannot wait to get back home. Jake
will have learned his lesson by now."

She remembered one time when she'd been having her hair
done, coming home and finding him in the kitchen baking a
cake of all things. When she'd confronted him about it, telling
him that it wasn't going to be good because it wasn't bought,
he'd told her it was for his grandma. It was her birthday or
something.

"Grandma loves strawberry cake. And I told her I'd make
one." Carol watched him as he spread the buttery icing all over
the thing. "You don't have to eat any of it if you don't want. But
I will. It's my favorite cake. What's yours?"

"Store bought. Not this.... Why on earth are you bothering
with that old bat anyway? She's not even nice to me, Jake. You
should just cut her out of your life so that I can be happy." He
just stared at her. "She's going to die soon anyway. If you cut
her out now, you won't have to think about anything but me."

"I love her." She told him it was a wasted emotion to love
someone as mean as her. "Grandma isn't mean to me."

"So you're implying that it's all me? That I've somehow
caused her to dislike me?" Jake didn't say anything, but
continued to ice the fucking cake. "Jake, I have never done a
damned thing to the old bitch. She's just not nice."

"You are forever mean to everyone." Carol asked him why
he'd say something like that. "Because it's true. We don't have a
staff because I can't afford to pay the type of people that would
be willing to work with you. You are even somewhat bitchy to

150

me."

Her anger, always so close to the edge, had her lashing out. Knocking the cake to the floor and hearing the bowl break made her feel wonderfully good. And when Jake looked at her, she could see his own anger and she was empowered by it. But all he did was get down on his knees and start to clean the mess up. She thought, right then, she hated Jake as much as she did anyone that had crossed her.

After that, it had been a game for her to see just how far she could push him. It never worked. He would just walk away from her, no matter what she said or did to him. And it had made her madder still that he'd not beg her to forgive him. So she'd left him, leaving him alone in the big house to see how he liked not having her around.

Frowning, she pulled up in front of her house. There were moving vans there, as well as large men who looked like they stank. She got out of her car and approached the one that looked the cleanest. Didn't men know that to smell was an abomination to mankind? She thought about giving him lessons on what was proper attire, too, when he turned and looked at her.

"I want to know what you think you're doing at my house." The guy just stared at her and she wondered if he was retarded. "I said, what are you doing to my house? I haven't given you permission to move things in here."

"I'm sorry, but I don't know who you are. We're working with Mr. Stout and Mr. Winslow." She told him Jake Winslow was her husband. "Oh. Well, I'm not sure then. We went to a place on Main, picked these things up, and were told to bring them here."

"I want you to stop taking this shit into my house, right now." The man didn't move to do as she told him. "Are you stupid as well as ugly? I said to stop taking things into my house. I have a set way things are to be put and standards that are high. None of these things are what I would put in a doghouse, much less my house. Now, have them take it all out."

Instead of doing as she wanted, he pulled out his phone. After pressing a few buttons, none of which she could see, he walked away from her. Just turned his back on her and walked away. No one did that to her, not anyone. But just before she reached out and snatched his neck, he held out his phone to her. He said it was her ex-husband.

"He's not my ex, damn it. I want you to stop saying that." Taking the phone from him, she growled low when she heard the laughter. People had better start being nice to her or she was going to have to make a few calls herself. "Jake. I don't care for what you think you're doing to my house. Who is this Stout person, and why would I want his things in my home? I have lovely things on order." He laughed harder. "You're beginning to piss me off."

"Really, because I thought you already were. When you killed your mother." Good, her first thought was, her mother was no longer a problem. "Your dad is dead as well, in the event that you're wondering. He killed Belinda then himself yesterday."

"Why would he do that? Christ, now what am I supposed to do? I thought he'd be thrilled that she was gone. Stupid man. Well, at least I'll inherit the money finally. Now I really can order all the things I wanted. But we have to clear up this problem with you moving someone's things into my home, Jake. I don't think you understand style at all." He didn't say anything and she assumed he was thinking of ways to make it up to her. "I need for you to reinstate all my credit cards now. We'll have plenty of money to cover my spending, what with my parents gone. Also, you'll need to write down some names for me. I want you to take them for all they have. People have been really mean to me today."

"Did you not hear me? Your parents are both dead. Murder/ suicide. They're dead." She waited for him to get to the point. Apparently he thought he'd made it.

"Jake, they're gone. I knew it was going to have to happen eventually. I mean, they were old and all. They just saved me the trouble of having to find a nursing home for them both. Really, this is much better." The men were still unloading the truck. "You should really talk to the man here. He has it in his head that he needs to finish this job and I want him to stop. Also, I'd very much like for you to come home. We have a lot of things to talk about. First of which is my credit cards and how you're going to make all this up to me."

"I'm not going to do any of those things. You and I? We're done." She started to tell him they'd be done when she said so, but he cut her off. "Those men are going to do their job, and you're going to leave them alone or so help me, Carol, I will have you arrested. Which, by the way, you might be anyway."

"For what?" He said that she'd beaten her mother to death. "No, you said that she was killed by my daddy. I had nothing to do with that. Besides, who really cares if she's dead or not? Not me. I'm thrilled to know that she won't be around to nitpick every little thing I do."

The line went dead and she threw it away from her. She was sick of this, people, especially Jake, acting as if she wasn't important to them. Damn it, she was married to him. He seemed to have forgotten that along the way.

Finding the man who she'd first spoken to, she told him to stop taking things into the house.

"I'm not going to do that. And don't think I don't know what you did with my phone there. Mr. Winslow, he's a good man, and you're shitting on his day." She asked him how this was her fault. "You're not married to him. Or won't be. You left that man in a lurch. You did the leaving, not him."

"Whatever." Since she couldn't get him to do as she wanted, Carol decided it was time that she did things on her own. Going into the back of the big truck, she was pissed because it was empty. Jake had done that, distracted her so that he could sneak in this other crap.

As she made her way to the house, she thought of all the color she was going to add just to the living room. The walls would be an eggshell so as not to distract from the color of the vibrant key lime color of the couch. The pillows would be a flush color, with bright spots of other colors. Even as she was thinking of the throws she'd have specially made for the room, two men stepped in front of her, blocking her way.

"I live here." Neither of them moved. "Look, guys, I'm not in the best of moods right now. But if you don't get the fuck out of my way, I'm going to hurt you both. And then call the police. This is my fucking home."

"Not according to the man we just spoke to." She asked

him who that might be. "Jake Winslow. He said to keep you from the house and to hold you down on the ground if need be."

"You most certainly will not. This is my home and I want you to get out of my way." She was getting really sick of this shit. "I swear to Christ; I'm going to own you when my husband is done with you. Get out of my way."

They backed her up. Carol was so mad when she found herself on the sidewalk in front of the house that she screamed at the top of her lungs. Several of the neighbors came out, most of whom had had nothing to do with her since she moved in. Glaring at them didn't make them scurry into their homes either. Carol was pissed. Then she heard the sirens.

"Good. Now we'll see who gets to keep me from entering my own home. Fuckers, all of you." As she stood there waiting, she started clicking off the things she was going to do now that she had more money. Jake would have to fork over a bit more than he had been willing to before. A lot more, as a matter of fact. She was so deep in thought that she was startled when the police were standing in front of her.

"I want you to arrest these pricks. They're blocking me from entering my home, and are putting furniture in there that I had no say over." She moved to the house again and was blocked again, this time by the men in blue. "I don't know what is up your asses, but I've had about all I can take of people being stupid around me. There are days when I think the entire world has gone fucking retarded. What the fuck is up your ass now?"

"Ms. Lane? We're going to have to ask you to come along with us. We have a few things to discuss with you about your parents." She said she wasn't Ms. Lane. "But you are. We have a warrant out for your arrest. Now, I would suggest that you come along...."

"You're not going to arrest me, you moron. I'm not going anywhere but into my home. And then I'm going to clean house. Quite literally. Everything in there is going to come out and get burned on this front lawn." Laughter had her turning, and she saw the men who had moved all that crap into her house watching from the front porch. Flipping them off, she turned back to the police. "Now, as I was saying, you are going to get the fuck out of my way before I have to hurt one of you. I just want to go in there and make plans."

"Your mother is dead. Your father too, did you know that?" She said that Jake had told her. "Did you hurt your mother, Ms. Lane? Before you left the house yesterday morning, did you hurt her?"

"Yes. So? She pissed me off." The officer looked at his partner then back at her. "What is it? I have shit to do."

"We're going to have to take you in, Ms. Lane. There are a few questions you have to answer." She jerked her arm from him when he touched her. "Ms. Lane, I'm going to cuff you if you don't come along peacefully."

Carol slapped him, hard enough to knock him back on the ground. Then before she could say a word, she found herself down on the ground as well, with someone sitting atop her. And no matter how many times she told him to remove himself from her person, he dug his knees deeper into her back. Then he jerked her arms around behind her and tied them together.

Someone was going to pay for this. Jake was going to be

very busy taking all these asses to court when she spoke to him. He might even let her have a limitless spending spree when she was finished with her list.

~~~

Jake hung up the phone and sat still. Several million things were running through his mind right now, and not one of them seemed to pause long enough for him to get a grasp on them to sort them out. He looked up when he heard someone say his name. Grandma was sitting there looking at him with the strangest look on her face.

"I take it you know." He asked her which thing that would be. "Carol has been arrested. She hit an officer at your home about an hour ago. They were taking her in to ask her about her mother's death when she turned on them. She's a fool if she thinks this is going to just go away."

"I know. I just heard. She's asking them to call me to come there and bail her out. I told them to lose my number." She told him good boy. "What else? I'm sure there is plenty."

"There is, but we'll talk about them one at a time. Not in any particular order, but we'll get to them. I spoke to Forrest. He said he was worried about you." Jake said he was fine. "Are you? You look a little freaked out. Is that a term to use in these kinds of situations?"

"I have no idea." She nodded. "Forrest said he was going to ask you to speak to his dad about dinner tomorrow night. Did you?"

"Oh yes. I had a great deal of fun with it as well. Did you know that at one time, Ranford Stout and his wife were employees of mine? I just remembered that when I saw his fat face an hour ago. He'll be there, by the way." Jake nodded. "Do you want to tell me why you're gathering the banes of your lives around you? Not me, of course, but the rest of them?"

"We were going to wait and tell you all at once, but I need to tell you now. Forrest and I think it would be better for you if we did." He told her what Forrest and he had found out. "So, my parents' not going to the wedding wasn't because they hated me or Carol; they weren't there because of the deal he'd made with Tyler Lane."

"What did they expect to happen? That she might kill you?" Jake said he had no idea. He was hoping to find out tomorrow night. "I see. And you're telling me early so that I can have my gun at the ready when he says he did it?"

"No. I wanted to tell you in the event that you didn't want to show up. It's going to be nasty." She said she had no doubt that it would be. "So, we'll understand if you tell me no. I wouldn't be there either if I didn't need to know what the hell they were thinking and why they did this to me."

"Money? Is there money involved?" He told her he would tell her at the dinner. "Forrest made some calls and got someone to take a peek, didn't he? I knew that he had some very talented friends that could do things less than above board. What are you going to say to him? And if I were you, I'd not go at this alone."

"No. Forrest is calling in a couple of his friends that are going to act as witnesses. There is also the new system that we're having put in the house. It was being put in before this thing with Father, just in the event that Carol showed up and tried something stupid. Which I guess she did." Jake leaned his head back and closed his eyes. "I feel like a rabbit in a hole. I mean, the night I came home and found my house devoid of Carol was the best thing I've ever had happen. And now it seems like everything that can go wrong has."

"But you met Forrest. That has to be something good." He looked at his grandma. "Honey, you'll get through this. I know you will. And once it's all over.... Good heavens. You're going to tell them all of it, aren't you?"

He laughed, the first one he'd had in a bit. "Yes, we're going to tell them that Forrest and I are lovers and that we're going to spend the rest of our lives making each other happy. If we can ever get things back to a reasonable state of normalcy."

"I don't think you'll want normal again now. And I'll be there. For the simple pleasure of seeing their faces when you tell them." She rubbed her hands together. "Jake, my boy, this is going to shake a lot of trees now. You see if it doesn't."

He hoped so. He really did. He was pissed off and exhausted. Not a good combination when it came to having long overdue conversations with his parents or his lover's father. Grandma told him that she was taking them out to dinner and that was final.

He called Forrest to let him know. Tomorrow they were going to come in and pack up his office here. Then he'd be moving his work to Stout and Winslow. Jake could not wait. And then that night, they'd have the dinner party of their life. He just hoped he'd get a chance to have some fun too.

CHAPTER 10

Thomas stood in the alley and waited. He knew that Forrest was in his office. There were enough people moving in and out of it that it had to mean that he was either going to be moving out or he was taking on a partner. He wondered who the fuck he thought he was going to play with now. When he finally saw him coming out with another man, he stepped in front of him. Thomas was a little pissed that Forrest didn't even look upset that he was there.

"Thomas. It's been a while. Not long enough, but a while. How the hell have you been? Oh, this is my lover, Jake. Jake, this is Thomas, the man I was telling you about." The other man didn't mean shit to him. "I thought you were warned to stay away from me."

"Nobody tells me what I can and can't do, Forrest. I want to know where my money is." He asked him what money that would be. "The money that you're going to pay me for keeping my mouth shut on what a prick you are."

"Oh? And how did you come to that conclusion? Not to mention, why do you think I'd pay you anything?" Thomas stretched his neck and was glad that it popped twice. Forrest had hated when he'd done that. But he wasn't playing right now. "I've moved on to much better things. You should as well. I'm not interested in any of your games any longer."

"What games? You prick, all you had to do was take it like a man and then I'd have the money I need. I have expenses, and you have made it extremely difficult for me to even get a date. What did you fucking do, call everyone you knew to be on the outlook for me? And what did you do to Vinny? The man is shitting bricks and won't even speak to me." Forrest looked at the man next to him. Thomas did as well. "You did this? You think that he's going to keep you around because you can pull a few strings and get me banned from the hangouts I go to?"

"I had nothing to do with you and your problems with your hangouts. And you've never yet said what he owes you for. Are you talking blackmail?" Thomas doubled up his fist and the man took a step back from him. "You take a swing at me and you and I are going to have some major issues. I'm not fucking around anymore."

"I have pictures." The other man said he didn't. "I do too. And you should have paid me off, not sent a vampire to talk to me. Now there are going to be troubles you never even thought of."

"Really? Because from where I'm standing, you don't have a pot to call your own. You living off the streets again, Thomas? Or have you moved into that vacant building on Tenth? I heard that it's full of rats and cockroaches. I'm thinking you'll fit right in with them." Forrest was well informed and that pissed him off more. "As for blackmailing me, you do know that's a crime, don't you? I mean, it really is something that I can take you to court over."

"Like I think you're going to do that. I know you're not telling people what a faggot you are. The great Forrest Stout is a mediocre lawyer and a fag. What do you think the local rags are going to do with that information?" No one said anything and that pissed him off more. "Stout takes it in the ass."

"So did you. And you screamed every time I did it too." Thomas wasn't prepared for him to be so calm. He wanted anger, for him to beg him to shut up. "It was fun while it lasted, but it's over. I think you should move on before you get hurt."

"You think you're going to hurt me? You mother fucker, you won't touch me. Do you want to know why?" He surprised him again by telling him that he did. "You won't touch me because I said so."

They looked at each other, Forrest and his lover. Then they burst out laughing. Thomas felt his head explode in anger, and his mind just leapt to killing the two of them. But before he could act on it, even if he had any idea how to, he was on the ground with his arm pinned up behind his back. And then Forrest knelt down and looked at him.

"My life partner has had a really shitty day so far. Well, a shitty week I guess. You might want to think about that when you hurl any more insults and try to hurt me." He called him a mother fucker again and screamed when he felt his shoulder pop. "I did warn you, Thomas. He'll hurt you more if you don't shut up and listen to me."

"You're going to pay. You fucking hear me? You'll pay for this shit." The pain in his shoulder was making him sick. He was gagging now, his belly not caring for what was being done to his body. "Tell him to let me go. Christ, he's killing me."

"I don't think anyone has ever died from a dislocated shoulder. Do you, Jake?" The man behind him laughed and said not that he'd heard of. "Yes, I didn't think so either. But there is always a first time."

"I'm begging you, Forrest. Tell him to let me go. Please?" He felt the pain in his arm lessen, then it seemed to take on a new form of pain. Thomas turned his head and threw up. Bits of it stuck to his mouth and he wasn't able to wipe it away. "You fuckers, I'm not going to forget this."

His head was jerked back. But instead of seeing Forrest there, it was the other man, Jake his name was. And he looked entirely too calm, looking at him like he was searching for a place to ram a knife. Then he spoke.

"As Forrest was telling you, I'm at my wits' end in dealing with people like you. First my soon to be ex-wife, my father and father-in-law, and now you. I'm holding on as tightly as I can, but you're really close to pushing the wrong button." Thomas was terrified. "If you keep this up, and a small part of me hopes that you do, I'm going to take every bit of my anger and frustration out on you. And I should warn you that I will not hold anything back in dealing with you."

He thought it was the calmness of the man, the way his voice never rose or lowered as he spoke, that scared him. Thomas had an idea that underlying that calmness was a person that could kill a man and not feel a single thing. He'd threatened a person, Thomas realized too late, that should never be fucked with.

"I'll leave the two of you alone. I swear it." Jake shook his head, like it was too little too late. "I swear it. You won't have to worry about me again."

"You see, I'd like to believe you. I really would, but sadly I do not. Neither does Quincey." Thomas asked who that might be. "Oh, you know him. Quite well as a matter of fact. He's the man who warned you to stay the fuck away from us."

A chill raced down his spine. He knew that the vamp was going to be involved in this. He just knew it. Telling them that he wasn't going to bother them again and again did nothing to change the looks on their faces. He was so fucked.

Then he was standing in front of him. The vampire.

"Hello, Thomas. I do hope that you've made all your personal arrangements." Thomas asked him what that was supposed to mean. "You've made out your will? Not that you have anything to leave anyone, but I find that I do want to know. Even if you did have someone that would care enough for you to call them a friend. But I'm finished with you and your ways. Bill Stalker was my friend too."

It took him several seconds to place the name. Bill Stalker had been his latest victim, a man that had fought back and lost. As Thomas was being lifted from the ground without either of the three men touching him, he started begging for his life.

"Don't kill me, please. I'm begging you. Please, don't kill me. He wanted me. What was I to do?" No one spoke, but the tightening around his throat was beginning to make him slightly lightheaded. "You're killing me."

165

"Well, of course I am. What did you expect?" He was down then, his knees hurting from biting into the concrete. Thomas stood; his plan was to run, but he felt sick, lightheaded again.

Then he felt it, the warmth of something being poured over him. Looking down at his chest, he saw the red stain begin to cover him. Reaching for his throat, he realized he'd been cut. And that he wasn't going to get any help from the men in front of him.

Staggering away, he fell on a woman. She hit him several times as he fell to the ground once again. Then she kicked him in the stomach as she screamed obscenities at him. Thomas held his neck, hoping to stop his life from being drained from him. But he had a feeling it was too late, much too late for him. Then Forrest was standing there.

"This is for the forty-three men you ruined because of what you did. For the lives ended when you went public with their secrets. There was no mercy from you, none when they begged you to leave them to their own misery." Then Jake was there, his face hard and set.

Thomas couldn't speak; he knew that he was dying. It wasn't right, wasn't fair that these men of all men were the last faces he'd see. As he faded out, because that was what it felt like to him, he thought of the man, Bill.

Thomas closed his eyes, thinking of the fun he'd had with the man a few days ago. How much money he had been going to get from him. Then he felt the first touch against his mind, a voice that told him it was Quincey.

He killed himself last night. Hung himself in his garage so that his wife would find him before his children did. The note he left her said that you had drugged him, raped him, and took pictures. Yes, he had done that, but he'd done that a hundred times before. What had made this one so different? *He wasn't gay. He had a good life, a wonderful family, and was loved by a great many people. And he was my friend. And you are going to pay with your life for taking something from him. His life.*

Thomas let his body go. There was no help for it. Not from anyone. He didn't feel regret, only in that he was dying so young. Smiling, or thinking that he'd like to, he let the weakness take him. Surely someone would come soon and help him. It was his last thought before he fell into what he hoped was a deep sleep.

~~~

Forrest wasn't sure how he felt about what he'd been a part of. Sadly, he felt very little. But he had stood there as a man's life was drained away. He wondered if Thomas had ever felt anything for him, ever. Or the countless other people that they'd not been able to find in their search.

"He deserved it." Forrest looked at Jake, who sat on the couch across from him. "Thomas was the worst kind of monster. He preyed on the kind of people that had no one to get help from. Or they thought they didn't have anyone."

"The police; did you know that Quincey messed with their minds, and they saw him as a self-inflicted gunshot wound?" Jake nodded. "And are you okay with that? That not only did we take part in his death, but lied about it as well?"

"How many people do you think are going to benefit by his death?" Forrest said that he had no money and nothing of value. "No, I mean the victims that he didn't touch, won't be able to. You know as well as I that there wasn't going to be an end to his treatment of others. That even though he said he'd leave people alone that he'd keep going back and back until this ended just the way it did. Not with his throat cut, but him being dead."

"I think so, yes. But that doesn't make it any easier to take. We watched a man die." Jake asked him if he'd seen a man die before. "No. I mean, I was there once when a client was put to death, but I didn't watch. It was bad enough that I had to be there."

"I did once. When I was about seventeen, two of my buddies and I were going on a trip. I don't remember where now, but we'd loaded up this old piece of shit van that belonged to one of them and set out. We weren't ten miles down the road when it broke down." Jake got up and moved toward him, kneeling on his knees at his feet. "None of us had any idea what might be under the hood of the thing, but we opened it. Just, I guess, to look manly. Anyway, there was a hissing sound and Fred decided it would be a good idea to open the radiator cap."

"Christ." Jake nodded. "I'm assuming from the start of your story, he was burned badly."

"Yes, but it didn't kill him. Sheppard, the other friend, he jumped back and was hit by a car. I mean, it should have been Fred; he was burned over sixty percent of his body. But Sheppard wasn't touched by the hot liquid. Instead, he was tossed up in the road and killed as I stood there and watched."

Forrest opened his legs when Jake moved between them. "I have no idea what your plan is, but our family is due here in about two hours. Not nearly enough time for whatever you have planned right now."

168

"I think I can make it work. Just don't touch me. You rush when you're needy." He did too, but put his arms on the back of the couch and held onto the cushions. "Forrest, you're going to let me explore and you'll behave."

"I'll try." Jake nodded. "But I'm not making any promises. You are just too much for a poor old man like me."

Jake was laughing when he unbuttoned Forrest's shirt. Forrest watched as he worked each little button out of the corresponding hole. The process seemed slow, methodical almost. Like he was working to make him crazy before he touched him.

When he had his shirt opened, Jake ran his tongue over his navel, his ribs. Forrest couldn't breathe, his body burned. Jake never touched him with anything but his mouth and his tongue. Forrest wondered briefly if when he did, he'd come.

His nipples were chewed on, nibbled enough that Forrest wanted to cup the back of Jake's head and hold him there. But he didn't touch him, didn't tell him to hurry, but enjoyed watching Jake explore him. He hissed out his approval when warm hands touched his ribs.

"Your muscles are so tight here." He nodded, not sure that he could stop himself from begging for more. "I can smell you. I never thought of a man smelling like sex, but you do. I love it."

"I can smell you too. When you come out of the shower, it's all I can do not to let my cat take me so that he can lick you dry. He wants to lick you someday." Jake said he'd love that and his cat purred along his skin. "Can you feel him?"

"I can. And someday I'll let him lick me until I come. But for now, this is my time." Forrest nodded, then cried out when

Jake swirled his tongue into his navel. He wasn't going to make it. Whatever Jake had planned was going to be cut short because he was so close to the edge. Rocking upward, trying to hurry him along without touching him, Jake moaned. "You're supposed to behave."

"I am, trust me. Because what I really want to do is throw you on the floor and fuck you." Jake's eyes darkened. His body pressed against his. Forrest rocked upward again and gripped the cushions harder. "I'm going to come all over you."

"Promise?" Forrest nodded and threw back his head and closed his own eyes when Jake touched his belt buckle. It was torture. Pure, complete torture.

Forrest heard the snap being released from its catch, the sound of the zipper moving over the teeth that held it closed. All this—Jake's heavy breathing, his heart pounding in his chest—made Forrest hungry for the man, starved to have him touch him, soothe while tearing him apart. And when a breeze, hot from Jake's mouth, blew over his hot hard cock, he looked down his body at him.

Nothing could have prepared him for what he saw on Jake's face. Love, yes, but there was so much more. Understanding. Compassion, as well as a plethora of every other emotion that one would have when on the threshold of so much.

Forrest wanted to touch him, hold him in his arms. He wanted to tell him that he couldn't live up to the love that he saw there. That it was impossible for him to be so happy. Forrest thought that should he die at this moment, his life would be complete. Then he realized that he had plenty of time to show Jake. Hours of conversations that they could share. Millions of minutes to be with him. For the rest of his life, Jake would be his.

Jake's mouth lowered to his cock. Forrest held his breath. And when he touched his tongue to him, circled his dark crown with it, Forrest cried out. It was too much and not nearly enough at the same time.

Jake fisted his cock, suckled his balls into his mouth. His hands were everywhere, fondling, touching him. When he felt his balls in his warm hands, Forrest closed his eyes again; there was only so much that he could see, hear, and feel.

Forrest hurt, his body so close to coming, because as surely as he lay there, being loved by his lover, he knew that it was going to be his body that came, not only his cock. And when he did, he'd be lucky not to faint dead away, it was going to be that epic.

Breathing became difficult. His heart was beating so hard, so fast, that he was sure it was going to leap from his chest. And when Jake told him to come, screamed for him to do so in his head, Forrest had no choice but to let himself go.

Coming had never felt this way. His toes curled, his hair tingled. Holding Jake now, his mouth wrapped around his cock, Forrest fucked him hard, coming not twice but three times as his body seemed to erupt with each release. Even as he felt the darkness take him under, Forrest knew for as long as he lived, he'd never forget this night.

When he woke he was alone in the big room. He could hear Jake in the other room, talking to someone. There were no other voices that he could hear, so he assumed he was on the phone. Standing up, he was slightly dizzy, weak really, and had to smile. He felt fucking fantastic. Pulling his clothing together, he sat back down to pull on his shoes and looked around the room.

Their furniture had blended well. Not only was the couch that Jake purchased post Carol the same one Forrest had in his own home, but the lamps were a perfect match to the floor lamp that Jake had. The pictures over the mantle had been the right size to fill the massive area. Since Jake hadn't purchased much else but a bedroom set and his living room things, Forrest's things filled out most of the rest of the house, including the dining room and the office that they'd share.

When he thought he could stand without making a fool of himself, he went to find Jake. He was in the main hall with his cell to his ear and his head leaning against the wall. He might have thought him upset but for the bursts of laughter that came from him. Forrest touched him on the shoulder, and Jake looked at him with tears in his eyes and humor, a great deal of it, on his face.

"I have to go, Grandma. I want to tell Forrest this before anyone gets here. You're coming early, right?" She must have said she was because Jake thanked her. "I'll see you soon. And thank you for this. You've made my entire day."

"I take it your grandma is enjoying herself with something." Jake nodded and told him she'd been talking to her son. "I bet that went over well."

"You have no idea. She said she called him to ask him about tonight's dinner and he said he wasn't coming. Last I heard he was. Anyway, she told him to get the stick out of his ass, her words, and to get over here. Because if he didn't, she was going to cut him off, and she didn't mean the money either." Forrest could see her doing it too. "I think she implied that she was going to hire a hit man to come after him."

"She knows a great many people, her relationship with Quincey notwithstanding. How did she meet him, do you know?" Jake told him. "You're kidding? She actually put an ad in the paper for a blood sucker to come and see her? Your grandma has some big balls. I think I'll be a little nicer to her from now on."

"You should call her Grandma like I do. But back to my dad. He said that he had no use for her money, and who else would she leave it to but to him? I guess he had it in his head that since he was her only son that he'd just inherit it all." Forrest knew that Jacob wasn't getting a dime of her money, that Jake was getting it all. "So when she informed him that she was going to live a lot longer than he was, he laughed. Grandma then told him about Quincey."

"You think that story she told before is true? That she is going to outlive us all?" Jake said he didn't know and apparently neither did his dad. "I love that old bat. She is the best woman I've ever known."

"My parents are coming but they're not happy about it. Your dad is going to be here, and is more pissed about it than my parents are. Grandma is taking bets on who leaves first and how they do it. Also, Carol is in jail, asking me to come in and bail her out. Then to represent her in her trial for killing her mother. This could not be more fucked up if you ask me." Forrest asked him if he was going to have fun. "You know, believe it or not, I'm actually looking forward to this. I think this is just what I need. What we both need."

"I agree. Once today is finished and we get this mess with Carol out of the way, then you and I need to figure out a nice place to go and take a long vacation. We can dust off our passports and have a nice long trip seeing other countries." Jake said that sounded fine to him. "Great. I'll work on that tonight, after they're gone."

"No, tonight you return the favor. You left me hanging."

As Jake walked away, Forrest started laughing. While he was in the bedroom getting cleaned up for dinner, he thought of all the things he was going to do to Jake. And he was sure it wasn't even going to come close to what he'd done to him on the couch. But he was going to try his best, even if it took him all night. Yes, sir, Forrest thought, life was going to be fucking perfect.

CHAPTER 11

Ranford wasn't happy. And more than that, he knew that whatever came of tonight he was going to be more pissed than he was at the moment. The nerve of his son telling Jenna Winslow to make him come here. And since she held all the cards right now, he either had to come here or be out on his ass. Fucking bitch.

His son moved about the room as if he owned it. He'd heard rumors that he had put his house on the market and was now living with someone. Ranford hadn't any idea what the new address was until now, and he wasn't happy about that either. Forrest was just trying to make him look foolish, and he'd pay for that as well.

"Would you like for me to make an announcement, Ranford? Or are you going to sit there and keep your mouth shut until you go home?" He glared at Jenna. "Don't you dare give me that look. Anyone with a bit of knowledge about the stock market and how to do a search can find out what I did in ten minutes. And I'm old. What did you think was going to happen when you started screwing with things you had no idea of?"

"I dislike you a great deal." Her laughter only fueled his anger. "I have no idea why you think that my coming here is going to make a bit of difference in whatever is going on here, but I'll have you know that I will not be blackmailed by you."

"No, I would imagine that you have enough of that going on in your life. When is the girlfriend due, Ranford? I think it's soon." He should have known that she'd find out that little tidbit of information as well. The woman was tenacious if nothing else. "I would have thought that after the first three times, you would have kept your Johnson in your pants and not out where any fertile woman could dance on it."

"The things you say sometimes border on obscene. What sort of people do you hang around with to learn such things?" She looked at his son and the man that he presumed to be his latest lover. "Him? He's nothing. Less than nothing. Had I known what he'd turn out to be I would have had his mother abort the monster."

"Are you referring to him being like her and a cat, or the fact that he's a homosexual? Either trait, as far as I'm concerned, is a good quality in a person." He said nothing. "I often wonder if you had any idea that Bernadine was a cat when you proposed to her. I'm thinking not. You think your blood is too pure to have mixed with her."

"She should have told me." Jenna only laughed. "Then when she told me that she carried my child, I worked my damnedest

176

to get her to leave it on the floor of a doctor's office. Even told her that I'd pay for her to have a nice long vacation, with no limit on how much she could spend." He looked behind him when she nodded to his right. His son stood there, looking at him with as much hate as Ranford had for him. "You can't have thought that you were welcome into my world. Your mother conspired against me, and in doing so, she was taken ill for life by giving birth to you. A monster."

"Monster or not, I'm a better man than you'll ever hope to be." Ranford stood up; it was time to take his son down a few notches. But almost as soon as he did, standing a good six inches shorter than his son, Ranford realized something else. His son wasn't the coward he'd been all those years ago. "What's the matter, Father? Have you only come to realize how much I look like you? Or is it the fact that I've grown up?"

"You sicken me. Here you are with this man, and what do you expect to get from it? Do you think he'll be friends with you when he figures out what a depraved mind you have?" He looked around the room for something else he could point out that Forrest would never have. "This place, I'm sure that it comes with a high rent. Did you come here thinking to show me how much you've come up in the world? I have news for you, Forrest, it was a waste of your money trying to impress me."

"I have no desire whatsoever to impress you. Not anymore at least. This house, along with the four thousand acres, belongs to Jake. My lover, my mate." Ranford looked at the man talking to the butler with new eyes. "In the event you missed it, Father, he's Jenna Winslow's grandson."

He felt his world crashing down around him. Forrest was mated? To a Winslow. He wanted to hurt him, lash out at him that it was lies. But he knew this was just the kind of thing that would happen to him, that his son would be richer than he was.

"You've done well then." Ranford wanted to go, to leave this place and never return. "I should be going." He turned to do so; his plans to come here and humiliate his son, to make him feel less than a person, were ruined.

"I've bought your loans." He turned slowly to look at Forrest as he continued. "Jake and I, we did some investigating and found that you're broke. Not just broke, but on the verge of being put out of your home. Isn't that about right, Father? You will be tossed out as well soon enough, when I get what I want from you. Then there is the money that you're paying out. My goodness father, you have been a very busy man."

"They're not mine." He asked him who. "Those bastards. They're not mine. I'm paying to keep them from going to the press. A man with my connections does not need this hitting the press about women just saying that I'm the father of their child. I'll deal with that soon enough too. However necessary. And I'm not broke...I'm in a financial bind, that's all. I'll be recovering before the ink dries on your next lawsuit."

Forrest sat down hard. Ranford wasn't sure what had happened, but was glad to see that he had felled him. But when he looked up at him, he could see contempt here, hatred like he'd never seen before.

"I was talking about the lawsuits from the vendors that you owe money to." The other man came to him, put his hand on his shoulder as Forrest stared at him. "You've fathered children that you're not acknowledging? I thought it was bad enough that you hated me, but to do that to a human child? How could you?"

"You make it sound as if I didn't do anything for you. Well, I have news for you. I did. You're not dead, are you?" Ranford stood up. "And I've had just about enough of this nonse—"

"Sit down." Ranford had no choice but to sit. The voice that thundered from his son made his cock shrivel in his pants and his head hurt. "You fucking bastard, you will not take this night from me. You will sit where I tell you to sit, speak when I allow it, and you will not, under any circumstances, leave this house without my permission. Do I make myself clear?"

Ranford nodded. He was terrified, more than he'd ever been. As he sat there, his body a mess of sweat, fear, and panic, he wondered where that had come from. Why the urge to roll to the floor with his belly exposed to his son had seemed not only the most natural thing to do, but there was an insane need to do so.

As other people came to this farce of a party, Ranford didn't move. It wasn't that he couldn't, he told himself, but he was comfortable where he was. No little shit of a faggot was going to tell him what to do. And when he saw Jacob and Trina Winslow coming into the room with him, he knew that his son was going to come out to them all, and he wanted to put a stop to it.

Standing up, Ranford hated that he found himself looking for his son. Not that he wanted to see him, but fear, the little finger of it, ran down his spine. When he made his way to the other couple, keeping an eye out for not just Forrest but Jenna as well, he asked to speak to them both alone.

"Dinner is served." He looked around the room when a butler, a big man, came into the room. And when he glared at him, like he knew he was going to cause trouble, fear came over Ranford. He wasn't even sure why.

The house was beautiful; he'd give that to the host. The room that they were led to by his son was huge, the table could have easily sat a dozen more people. There were chargers on the place settings with name tags that were done in a lovely hand, as well as several wine glasses per setting. Ranford just knew this was going to be one of those faggy dinner parties with all kinds of food that he didn't know what the fuck he was eating.

He wasn't going to eat any of it. The decision made, he leaned back in his seat and didn't even bother picking up his napkin to lay over his lap. It was in his head to tuck it in his shirt like he was five years old, but he decided that ignoring the shit in front of him was easier.

When the young man stood up — Jake, he thought his name was — the room grew silent. But only for a moment. Jacob told him to sit down and then Jake nearly did. Then Trina started crying, loud wailing noises that hurt his head.

~~~

"What the hell do you think is happening here? I told you to sit down." Jake stiffened his entire body for the onslaught of words from his dad. "When I tell you to do something, Jake, I do not expect any lip or excuses. And you might as well know that I've called in a few favors, and you will not be divorcing Carol Lane. I don't care what you think she did to you, or even

180

if she actually did. You will not divorce her."

"She's going to prison for the murder of her mother. Does that change your mind about the divorce? I know that appearances are everything to you and Mother." His dad looked around the room and glared at his grandma. "You think she had something to do with this?"

"You and she are like two peas in a pod. Always conspiring against us. Well, I will tell you right now that I won't stand for it. I'm done with the lot of you." When Jake's father stood, so did Forrest. "What do you think you're going to do to me? Turn me into what you are? I've had people like you killed for less."

"No doubt you have. But we're not done here until he says we are. Now, you fat mother fucker, sit down before I knock you down." His dad tried hard to not do as he'd been told by Forrest, but in the end he sat. And like Ranford, he shoved his plate away as well. "You people might want to pay attention here. This will more than likely be the last time you see either of us."

"Good." Jake wondered if it hurt Forrest when his father spoke. But it didn't appear to. Then he looked at his own parents and thought he might be better off with them completely out of his life as well.

"As I was saying, Carol is going to go to prison for the murder of her mother. Before her father killed himself, he had been told that there had been no brain activity for Belinda. Killing her when he killed himself was not murder. Carol did that for him." He looked around the room to the people that, for the most part, meant little to nothing to him. His grandma and Forrest were all he had. "I've decided to leave my partnership with the firm, and I'm moving my practice in with Forrest. We'll be taking on—"

"You most certainly will not." His father stood up and slammed his fist on the table, breaking two wine glasses. "You will stop this right now, Jake. I will not sit here and let you ruin all that I've sacrificed just to see you ruin my reputation with this queer."

"Really? I wasn't aware that you had any say over what I did and didn't do. Not for a very long time. And tell me, Father, what sort of sacrifices have you made for me? You talked about conspiring? Did you mean when you and Tyler threw Carol and me together? Was it your plan for her to kill me one night in a fit of rage so that you could draw the insurance you had put on me? Or was it the money that Tyler gave you on the day of the wedding and every two weeks since to take her off his hands?"

"What?" Jake glanced at his grandma when she stood up. "What is this? Jacob, what have you done?"

"Nothing that any other man wouldn't do for a son that he could not stand nor want. I did this for my family." Grandma asked his dad what family that would have been. "You cut me off until you die; what the hell was I supposed to do for that money? Had you just gone on like a normal mother and died when you were in your seventies, then I'd not have had to resort to filling my coffers another way. It was working too. I will not have this thing you see as a problem end that either. For as long as there is money in the estate, no matter what, I get my cut. So long as they're married. It's only right that I should."

"You're a sick bastard, Jacob. I never knew that until just

now." Grandma looked at him when she continued. "Go on, Jake…tell him the rest. I'll be in the living room with my friends."

Attorneys. Grandma had brought in a slew of them for this dinner tonight. Forrest had told her that now that he was in a relationship with Jake, he could no longer help her, and she understood. He wondered what his father was going to do now, after tonight, when all money was cut off. He turned to his father.

"I've left the firm as of this morning. My divorce is final due to Carol's status, and I'm coming out of the closet, I guess you could say." He took Forrest's hand as he continued. "Forrest and I are lovers, and will remain together until death us do part."

The explosion was long in coming. But when it erupted, Jake wasn't sure if he wanted to laugh at his parents or simply cry. His mother started her bawling again, fat tears that rolled down her cheek almost comically. His father started screaming at him, pounding his fist against the table and calling him names. Jake just let him.

He'd come to the conclusion that he was an adult. Yes, he supposed that he'd been one for a very long time, but being happy and in love had given him a great deal more confidence than anything he'd ever done before. Frankly, Jake thought, he just did not give two fucks what people thought anymore.

Jake realized that things had gotten quiet as he'd stood there letting the arguing and sobbing roll over him for a few moments. He burst out laughing, his entire body feeling like it had been given a large dose of some happy drugs. Then he looked around the room.

Finding his dad on the floor with a huge tiger on his chest, his mouth around his throat, wasn't really funny, Jake thought. As he moved closer to them, his lover and father, he noticed two things at once. The gun, and then his grandma.

"What have you done?" He went to her, lying so very still on the floor, and knew that she was dead. There was a neat hole in her forehead, and blood pooling around the carpet surrounding her. "Father, what did you do?"

Picking up her hand, Jake felt his world crash down around him. His grandma, the only person that had ever loved him no matter what, was gone. He looked at his mother as she sat on the floor near his father, and wanted to take the gun and end them both. They'd done this, taken her away from him.

Jake, I need for you to call the police. He nodded at the voice in his head, getting some comfort from the sound of Forrest's voice. *Come on buddy. You need to get up and make the call. And to tell the others in the living room what has happened.*

I don't know what happened. Forrest asked him again to call the police and to tell them that his grandma had been shot. *All right. But you'll tell me then?*

Yes. Your father wasn't happy that you were doing things on your own. He said that if you were going to try anything that he didn't approve, then he wasn't going to allow you to live. Jake pulled out his cell phone and called the report in. Then he made his way to the living room as Forrest continued. *You seemed to be smiling at him, and I think he took that as you doing as you damned well please. Him pulling a gun out startled all of us into a stupor, and when he pointed it at you and fired, your grandma just jumped in front of you. There wasn't any time for anyone else to react, it was over in a split second.*

Jake told the two men in the living room what had happened. That his grandma had been shot by his father and that she was dead. He sat down on the couch when they left the room, pulling out their cells as they went. Jake just needed to be alone.

I'm going to our room to change. You should know that Quincey is here as well. He's not saying much, but there is an aura around him that is glowing with anger. Jake said to let him kill his father. *I can't do that, and you know why. The man has to be prosecuted. To the fullest extent.*

I know, but that doesn't mean I have to be happy that he gets to live. Forrest said nothing. *He was going to kill me. My own father was going to kill be because I'm happy.*

That's about right. Saying it was one thing, having it confirmed was something entirely different. It really brought it home. *You're going to be just fine, Jake. I promise you this.*

I loved her. With all my heart. She was the only woman in the world who ever loved me, held me when I needed it, and slapped me around when I needed that as well. He heard the sirens but didn't move. *Forrest, what will happen if Father says a cat hurt him?*

It won't matter at this point. He's as good as convicted. Jake knew that as well. But he told Forrest he was still worried. *Don't be. Anyone else in that room is going to say that they never saw anything. My dad will talk, but all I need to do with that is bring up the fact that he was getting back at me. Also, there are his past complaints about my mother being the same thing. It'll mean nothing in the long run.*

And my mother? What will happen with her? He didn't reply and Jake sat there, just wondering what his mother had done now. He could feel Forrest, his emotions, but not what it was he was feeling. Anger? Sympathy? Whatever it was, Jake figured he'd find out about it later.

"Mr. Winslow?" Jake turned to the voice, not understanding for a moment that it was a person talking to him and not a voice in his head. "Mr. Jake Winslow?"

"Yes." He stood up and faced the officer. "I'm sorry. I came in here...I'm not entirely sure why I came in here. To breathe, I think. I don't know. My grandma is dead."

"Yes, we're talking to the others in the room now." He came more into the room. "You should know that I'm not human. Forrest knows me, but I wanted to tell you that so you'd know you could tell me the truth about what happened."

Jake reached to Forrest, not sure who to trust.

Yes, tell him everything. What he needs will go into his report, the rest will be set aside for later. He's the pride leader, as well as a cop here in town. Jake started to ask him what that meant when he answered him. *Like I said, he's the pride leader. If there is trouble with this, I could face some fines. He told me not to worry but for you to tell him the truth. It'll be all right.*

Sitting back down, he offered a seat to the cop. Jake told him everything that he knew, even some of the things that he could only guess at. Then he got to the part where he'd found his Grandma lying in a pool of her own blood.

"Forrest said that he attacked your father because he was fearful of him killing you as well." Jake said he didn't know, but could see his father and Forrest doing just that. "You think

186

your father meant to kill you?"

"Yes. I had just told him that Forrest and I were lovers and that we're going to be living here. And I also mentioned that I had left my firm to work with Forrest as well." The man nodded. "I'm sorry. I don't know who you are other than the leader of the pride here."

"Frank Carlson. My wife, Lila, and I don't live too far from here. Not in this nice of a home, but we're happy there. Are you?" He said that he was now that he was living it the way he was. "Good. I'm glad to hear that. I've met your ex-wife, by the way. She's a real peach, isn't she?"

"More like the pit." He laughed when Jake did. "She's in jail; I'm assuming that's where you might have met her."

"Yes. She and I have had words over some things. She's a woman used to getting her own way, I think." Jake said that she was. "When your father pulled the gun, where were you standing?"

"Across from him. He was talking, yelling at me really, when I sort of zoned out. I was thinking about how happy I was, and that pissed him off." Jake didn't have trouble keeping up with the conversation's switches. "Carol killed her mother, I'm sure you know that."

"Yes. We were there when the doctor told Mr. Lane that his wife would have no quality of life in her current condition. He asked him if he wanted to donate her organs, other things while she laid there, but he said no, said he wanted her whole when she was buried." Frank looked at his notes. "The attorneys said that they'd been called here to make changes to Mrs. Winslow's will. Did you know that?"

"No. I thought they were here to talk to my father. I guess he's been complaining about the amount of money my grandmother had been giving him. Something about investments, and I think she wanted them here to make sure that he didn't do or say anything stupid." He looked at the door where he could hear the others talking. "I guess he did. He killed her."

"Yes. I'm sorry." Jake nodded. "One more thing, Jake. When your father shot at you, when he fired the weapon, do you know if he had it with him or did he get it from here?"

"I don't have guns in the house." He nodded and waited. "No, he came here with it as far as I know. I remember vaguely, in a distant sort of way, seeing him pull it from his jacket pocket. But not much else."

"Did you know that he carried a gun? The reason I'm asking is, the gun is registered to your mother." Jake said he didn't know. "What can you tell me about your mother, Jake? Do you know what happened to her?"

"Something happened to her?" He nodded but said nothing more. "I can't tell you for certain, no. Mother had some issues. I have no idea if she suffered from depression or if crying all the time got her anything she wanted. I had become immune to it. But as for today, no, I can't say that I know where she is now. She was in the dining room too."

"Your mother is dead." Jake said nothing, not even sure what he could say at this point. "Do you want to know how?"

"I can honestly say that I don't care. I mean, I know that sounds like I'm a cold hearted prick, but after today, I just can't muster up any kind of sadness for her or my father." Frank nodded and stood up. "Is Forrest in trouble?"

"Why would he be?" Jake asked about shifting in front of humans. "There wasn't a person out there that doesn't have some knowledge of shifters in general. But as for him shifting to save your life, no one outside the pride will believe that he did such a thing. And even if it hits the papers, who is going to believe anyone in that room? No one, I can tell you that. Forrest is just fine."

Jake knew that at some point he was going to have to leave the living room. He wasn't in any kind of hurry to do so. When Forrest came to sit with him, neither of them said a word as they held hands. Things were just too intense right now for them to speak.

CHAPTER 12

Carol paced the little cell. Why she wasn't given a bigger area was beyond her, but they said she wasn't going to be moved or her room enlarged. Not that she had any idea why she was in here, but some officer told her that she was going to stay until her trial. Carol wanted her husband there.

She heard someone coming through the doorway to the area she was in. There were other people around. None of them as important as her, she knew this, but they seemed to have lots of people coming to see them. When an officer stood in front of her cell, Carol didn't even bother standing up. He would put out the nasty food then come to get it in an hour, he'd tell her. It was the way he did things.

"Ms. Lane?" She told him for the millionth time it was not Lane, but Winslow. "Yeah, that's why I'm here. There is an attorney here to see you. He'd like to talk to you about your divorce. But he said he won't if you don't behave yourself this time."

"Where is Jake, my husband?" He only rocked back on his heels. "You are the most annoying man I've ever met. I want you to tell Jake where I am and that I need him to come here and get me out. I have to get to my house."

"You're not going to get out any time soon, and he's a little busy right now. There has been a shooting at his home." Carol told him it was her home and asked about the walls. "I'm not sure what you mean. What about the walls?"

"Were they damaged? When I have things repainted when I get home, I need to know if the walls were damaged. They'll have to be fixed before the painters can come in. I think my husband might have had the walls redone, but they won't be right." He said nothing but stared at her. "I asked you a question. Are the walls damaged from any sort of blood or bullet holes? These are things I have to know."

"Mr. Winslow, Jake's father, shot and killed his mother. I guess he was aiming at Jake, but I don't know the particulars on that right now." She asked about Trina. "I'm afraid that she's dead as well. Cut her wrists in the bathroom when she was told her husband was being taken away."

"She didn't like me either. And with Jenna gone, Jake and I will inherit that old bitch's money as well. We're going to be so rich." She was trying to think how much money that might be with her daddy's money, and looked at the police officer when he cleared his throat. "Is someone else dead that you know of?"

"No, ma'am, not that I can tell right now. You do know that these people are your relatives, right? That Jenna Winslow was a wonderful woman who was well thought of. Mrs. Winslow wasn't nice, but she is still a person that is dead." Carol asked him why she should care about them. "They're all dead."

"Yes, I'm aware of that now. Thank you for telling me. Do you think that someone could bring me a phone? I need to set up painters and workers to move into the house now. The downstairs powder room is going to be a challenge. I think people will just want to come over to use it just because they'll know that someone died in there." She started pacing again, her mind working on how to best use this to her advantage. "I could play it up a bit. Have the walls sponged in a nice dark red to highlight the things in the room. Perhaps I can use some of the crime scene photos on the walls. What do you think?"

"I think you need to realize how cold you sound right about now. Don't you think people will think you're strange for not getting at least a little upset about any of this?" She asked him why they would. "Because not only are both your parents are dead, one of them by your hand, but your in-laws are too."

"Okay, first of all, Jenna was a royal bitch. Not to mention like eight hundred years old. She looked good for her age, but she had to go sooner or later, and now suits Jake and me better. My mother was a nag and she was kicking me out of their home. Not to mention she really held Daddy back from things. I think she was the main reason that he didn't treat me as well as he should have." She thought about Trina. "Jake's mother wasn't really a bad person, but Christ, she was depressing as fuck to be around. Crying all the time. Whining about this or that. I just couldn't stand her, and maybe, had I really thought of it, I might have helped Jacob out with her like I helped my daddy."

He looked around and she noticed that he was looking at

the camera there. Carol had no idea if it worked or not. She wasn't worried about it, however. There were more important things going on than a stupid camera that might be recording her naked or something. She asked him when Jake was coming in.

"I don't think he is. I'm pretty sure that he has enough on his plate right now without coming to see you. Tell me again why you think you did your daddy a favor by taking care of your mom." She asked him if he meant by killing her. "Yes, I guess so."

"I didn't, you know. Kill her, I mean. I just beat her up really badly. She should have died, I guess. I lost my temper again." He asked her about that. "Oh, when I was younger there was this couple that took the last ticket to a movie I wanted to see. I asked him really nicely to give it to me—I am Carol Lane, after all—and he gave me this sob story about how it was his and his wife's anniversary and that they'd saved and planned this night for ages." She snorted. "I didn't have to save, I had the money right on me. So when he didn't give it over, I had to hurt him for it. I think his wife was hurt too…died, I think. And you want to know something? I didn't even get to see the flipping movie. The police took me downtown and in one of these cells."

"Then what happened?" She asked him what he meant. "You didn't go to prison. You never had a trial. Why is that?"

"Oh. Daddy. He handed out money all the time when I messed up or got caught." The officer asked her how many times she'd messed up. "Well, if you don't count Mother, three times. I only meant to make them understand me, but this guy just didn't want to do things my way. Then there was the teacher at the school. That's when Daddy bought me Jake."

"Excuse me?" Carol looked at him. "Your dad bought Jake? You mean he paid him off for something?"

"No. Jake's daddy sold him to my daddy. For a lot of money too. I'd been in trouble, again, and Daddy said it was marry me off to change my name or I was going to have to move away. I had seen Jake at a friend's party and I knew that I could get him to do things the way I wanted, so I told Daddy that I wanted him." She smiled at the officer, thinking this was sort of fun, telling him about how wonderful her daddy had been. "So when he went to Jacob to tell him what he wanted, Jacob said he wanted money. A lot of it. Something about being ashamed of his son for something in college. Anyway, Jacob signed his son over to my daddy, who gave him to me. I need him here. Do you think you can get Jake to come here? He is mine, and I need him to come here."

"I'll work on that."

When he walked away, Carol thought of the other things her daddy had given her when she'd married Jake. Money, sure, but that didn't last long. He was also supposed to make sure that she and Jake got everything they wanted when they wanted it. But he never did that. Not even giving her credit cards when Jake had told her no. Her mother had caused that, she knew it. Carol decided right then and there that when she and Jake were back together, he was to never say that word to her again.

It was getting dark again, and one more night in this place wasn't in her plan. And she realized that no one had brought her a phone either, or a computer. How the hell was she supposed to order things for her new home when no one was helping her? She'd have to get someone to help her or she'd never have the house done by Christmas again. That was the time to show off, she knew.

She was just getting up to bang her shoe on the bars that held her in when she saw a man coming toward her. Carol thought it was Jake, but there was something different about him. Then she noticed the man with him.

"I know you." He bowed before her and she had to smile. This was the way to treat a woman. "If I wasn't married to Jake here, I'd get someone to make you marry me."

"Not on your ever loving life would I even entertain the thought of touching you, much less wedding you." Carol wasn't sure if he'd just insulted her or not, so decided not to ask. "You requested for Jake to be here. And as his attorney, I'm going to advise him on what to say to you or not."

"Why would you care if he spoke to me about things? Not that it matters, I guess." She turned to Jake. "You have to pay them off so that I can get home. I want to get the house ready for the holidays. And I do hope that you got rid of that ugly stuff you brought in when I was gone. Jake, you have no sense of style at all."

"You're not coming to my home again, Carol. I think I made that perfectly clear when I filed for divorce." She waved him off and told him to be serious. "I'm dead serious. I'm not going to allow you to be near me, much less in my home."

"Jake, I'm not sure why you're treating me this way, but I won't stand for it. I want you to go give those people whatever it takes to release me. Mother and Daddy are both gone now, so it's not like you don't have the cash to settle things up for us." Jake just stood there. "Oh, you can't say anything in front of your lawyer. I get it. Just send him away and we can make plans. I have so much to do. Did you know that they won't even give me a phone in here? You'll have to give me yours so that I can get some things done while you're working on the rest."

"I'm not going to get you out of here. I'm certainly not going to give you a phone, and when you're convicted of murder, you won't be able to inherit anything from the estate either." She asked him why she'd be convicted of anything. "You killed your mother, Carol. That's why."

"Oh no, you have that wrong. Daddy killed her. I just beat her up. I thought she was dead or close to it when I left her on my floor, but Daddy pulled the gun on her." Carol was starting to get aggravated. "Jake, I don't have time to sit here and debate this. Just pay them off so I can get home. You have a lot to make up for when we get there. And I've decided that there will be no more telling me no. I don't care for that word at all."

"No." She stomped her foot. "No, I am not going to bail you out, even if there was bail set for you. No, I'm not giving you my phone so you can order whatever is in your sick mind to do to my home. And I will most certainly tell you no, that you are not ever going to have me pay anyone off for a dammed thing you do from now on. You are on your own."

"Daddy said you were to take care of me. This is not taking care of me at all, Jake. Get the fucking money here and get me out of this place. I'm much too smart and pretty to be locked up like this." He crossed his arms over his chest and stared at her. "You're really starting to piss me off. Do what I say now or else."

"Or else what, Carol? Are you going to hurt me?" She said that she would. "Well, that's the reason you're in here. You're not getting free. You're going to prison."

"I don't want to go to prison. Damn it, why are people being so fucking mean to me?" She wanted him to answer her, but he looked over at the man next to him. He was smiling that sort of smile that didn't go all the way to the eyes. "Who the fuck are you and why are you here? There is no reason for Jake to need a lawyer. Go away."

"No. Wow, that word is pretty nice to use when someone tells you not to use it, isn't it?" He laughed. "I'm here, as I told you, to advise Jake. Not that I think he needs it, but in the event you get stupid...or in this case, stupider. Also, it's because I want to see your face when he tells you of our good news."

"What good news? And Jake, don't think I've not noticed that you've not given me your phone yet. I have some places to call before I move back in with you, so I want to get a good start on those places in the morning." He just stood there. "You have no right to treat me this way. My daddy said you'd be a sap and do what I want when I want. Well, you're not doing anything like you should."

"And I won't either. I wanted to come here to tell you, first of all, that my grandma has been murdered." She tapped her foot. "You really are a cold, heartless bitch aren't you? Anyway, I've also found someone to love. For the rest of my life."

"Who? No one that I know would dare touch what is mine. Jake, you're not marrying material, you know that, don't you? I mean, I hate to break it to you, but you are a dumbass, as well as a prick at times. No one is going to ever love you." She smiled at him. "Did you hear me? I said that you're not going to find someone to love you, not unless they want to be dead too."

"I'm his lover." Jake smiled at the man, a smile that not only reached his eyes but seemed to be a part of his body. Carol looked at the other man and asked him what he was talking about. "Jake is my lover. We're partners."

"In your law firm." He told her that as well. "I don't understand. Lovers? You mean you like him. That the two of you are going to be law partners."

"We're lovers as in being in love with each other. We're going to live together as lovers, die together as them as well, I guess. And yes, we're also law firm partners." Carol was still confused. "Jake and I are gay."

"No. I don't think so. No, he's my husband and I'll say what he is or not. And he's not gay. I won't have it." The man laughed again. "Look, I don't know what sort of games you're playing here, but Jake is my husband, not some lover of yours. Not that he'd do that sort of thing, but he belongs to me. Daddy said so."

"Well, your father is dead and I'm gay. A homosexual. And Forrest is my mate." She stepped back from the bars, shaking her head. This wasn't right. "And when you go to trial next week, I'm going to testify against you. By the way, the courts granted me an early divorce due to the fact that you're a murderous bitch, and as your ex-husband, it's my right to go on living without you interfering in my life; my new one."

"You think you're happy now, you just wait." She looked at the two of them and noticed that they were holding hands.

"Let him go. What is wrong with you? Do you want someone to see you like this? Daddy would be appalled. Christ, Jake, what will the neighbors think?"

"I don't care what anyone thinks anymore. And I certainly don't give a fuck what you think. I only came here to let you know that as of this very moment, I'm done with you." She told him that he wasn't until she said so. "You see, Carol, that is where you're wrong. I don't need you in my life, nor do I need your permission for anything I might do. Believe it or not, I'm a grown man who can and will make my own decisions."

When he turned to walk away from her, she saw red. The fucker wasn't going to get off that easily, and Carol told him to get back there. He just kept walking, holding hands with that other man.

"Jake, when I get out of here, you're going to pay for this. I'm serious, you're in deep shit with this, and I won't have you embarrassing me like this. Get back here right now, you fucker. Jake, come back here." When she heard the door shut she felt sick to her stomach, she was so angry. As she made her way to the bed again, she nearly screamed when she saw a man standing in the corner. "Who the fuck are you? You know, I don't care. If you can get me out of here, I'll pay you whatever you want. My daddy was rich."

"I don't care." He moved to her, close enough that she had to step back or he'd touch her. But he still did, running his fingers over her cheek to her throat. "You're such an ugly person, aren't you? Inside and out. I will enjoy this, I think."

"I don't want you here." Her blood was pounding in her ears and she could almost taste her own fear. "How did you get in here?"

"I can move very quickly and transport myself wherever I want to go. And even though I'd rather not be here, I think I must be." He wrapped his fingers around her throat, and even thought it wasn't tight, she could feel her breaths being cut off. "You are going to do just what I tell you, Carol Lane. I have no desire to have you turning up in the lives of my friends again and destroying their happiness."

"I don't know what you mean. Let me go." She stood there, her body stiff with fear as he took her sheet from her bed. "What are you doing?"

"Tear this into strips for me. They don't have to be even, just nice ones that you can use. Do it." It was as if she had no choice. Taking the sheet from him, she started tearing it into strips. "Very good. Now tie the ends together into a long rope."

"I don't want to." He only smiled at her and she fell backward. "You have fangs. I can see them; you have.... Are you a vampire?"

"I am indeed. I'm not going to tell you again to make a rope. I shall have to kill you myself if you don't comply. And you need to suffer for the lives that you've ruined. Don't disobey me again, Carol Lane, or I will end your miserable life."

Carol did as she was told. Not that she knew why she was doing it, but she did. And when she had all the pieces together, she held it to her like a long blanket. He took it from her and slipped it over the top railing of the bars. Just raised up and wrapped it there.

"What do you think I'm going to do with that? It's not going to free me." He told her that in a way it would. "I'll be able to go to my home? I have a lot of work to do there."

"You'll not have to worry about that at all. But I do have something to tell you. A promise I made to a dear friend of mine. Would you like to know what it was?" Carol told him that she didn't care to hear about his friends. "Too bad. Jenna told me that should she die before you went away, that I was to come here and take care that you never got out to bother Jake again. She made me promise her that, even though I would have done it anyway. So here I am, fulfilling a promise to someone I loved dearly."

"Jenna hated me." He laughed at her. "Look, my daddy was really well off. If you just walk away now, I'll give you a lot of money. Jenna is dead. It's not like she'll know if you did it or not anyway."

"I'll know. And I have no use for your money. I have more than even you could spend in several lifetimes." He told her to wrap the rope around her neck. "Do it, Carol. The hour grows late, and I need to be gone from here."

Carol wrapped the rope around her neck. Even stood up on the bed where he told her to. It wasn't right, him doing this to her, but she knew that in the end she'd win out. She was Carol Winslow, after all, and was now very wealthy. When he stood back to look at how she was positioned, Carol tried once more to get him to set her free.

"I'll even let you fuck me. I don't care for you, but if you'll let me go, I'll let you fuck me. Any way you want." He laughed. "I'm not being funny here."

"Oh, but you are. To fuck you, as you so crudely put it, would be the worst thing to happen to me. And trust me when

202

I tell you that I've fucked some pretty disgusting things in my life." He laughed again. "Yes, that would never do. Now be a good little human and wrap the rope around your neck so that I can see you pay."

The rope was heavy; her body felt leaden by what she was about to do. No amount of begging would make him stop this. No matter how much she offered him he turned her down. This wasn't right. She had things to do.

"Stand on the bed there and I'll help you out." She told him no and he touched his finger to her cheek again. "You have no choice in the matter, Carol. Your crimes, all of them, deserve a good justice. And I'm here to make sure there is one."

He told her to step off the bed, and when she did the bulkiness of the rope tightened. Her air was getting harder and harder to suck in. She began to claw at the rope, trying her best to take it away, if only to loosen it so she could breathe, but the vampire told her to put her hands down.

Bright sparks of light began to blind her. Her chest hurt, her neck burned. Then as she was ready to close her eyes, she opened them when the man said her name. It took a great deal of focus to hear him.

"I shall see you in hell, Carol Lane." Carol closed her eyes then, thinking that was just too much. Then nothing.

CHAPTER 13

Quincey sat on the swing. He'd been there for over an hour, his body just swaying back and forth as if he had not a care in the world. He supposed in a way he didn't. Life, he'd come to realize, was a bit too much for him, and he was ready to face his immortality full on. When the swing took a violent twist, he looked at the man sitting beside him.

"Did you know that if you sit here long enough and quietly enough, all manner of things come out to play?" He said nothing as they moved the swing back and forth no faster than a breeze might do. "I heard that you've been avenging the death of a great many people. How does that set with you?"

"I have had enough." The swing moved again. The same motion that he'd felt with his own sanity of late, highs and lows. "Did you come here to tell me that I am to die? If you would grant me a single request, I shall go with you quietly. Without any trouble."

"Nay, I have come to talk to an old friend." Quincey nodded. "What if I told you that what you have done of late has been with the approval of the council? That no one cares one way or the other how they have died, only that they have?"

Quincey said nothing but continued to swing with his friend. He'd been instrumental in a great many endings the last few days. Most of them had been at his command, others just a word here or there.

"Trina would never have survived without her husband. Jacob would have given in to his daughter-in-law's demands and either had Jake killed or destroyed. He got all that he deserved." He thought of Jenna and her death hurt him badly. "Had I to do it over again, I don't think I would have changed a thing. Only the death of my dearest friend, which I would have prevented had I known."

"You would have been hurt too." Quincey told him that he was already. "Yes, I can see that. Feel it as well. But it was what was needed. A good woman; she was the best, but her death has made a great many things move in the right direction."

Quincey saw the young tiger in the woods. Then he saw Jake, naked, running in the opposite direction. There was no fear between them, no anger in their hearts. Just two lovers having a grand time despite the sorrow in their hearts. He wished that he could be so carefree.

"Jenna left them everything. She told me that it was the way that it should be. I have her things, her paintings and her books. It was more than I thought I deserved from her." He thought of the conversation that he'd had with young Jake about them. "He told me that she would have wanted me to have them, assured me that she loved me as much as I did her."

"Yet you did not tell her. Or him, did you?" Quincey said that it wasn't the time. "Nay, not any longer. I wish for you to do me a favor. It will not cause you any hardship, and you may say no if you do not want to do it. As I said, it is only a favor."

"I wish to end this life, you know that. It's why you are here. But if this favor you ask of me is to not do that, then you are wasting your breath. I have better things to do than to chase after small things for you to keep me alive." Quincey looked at the man he'd known longer than trees on this ground had been here. Longer than the lake that now ran along the property was anything but a small trickle from the stones above. "To come here, when I have been to the grave of my only child, is cruel even for you."

"Jenna came to me. Weeks ago, and asked me to care for you. I told her that you were a grown man, a man with strange ideas and even stranger ways. She assured me that if anyone could do this for her, it would be me." He looked over at him and Quincey felt his heart hurt for his lost child. "She knew, I think, that I was your sire. The man that made you what you have come to hate."

"I have never hated what I am. Only what I could not do." He looked out beyond the field and wondered at the men there. At his great-grandson that might well carry a part of him. "Jake has a part of me inside of him. It will only take a touch to give him all that I have."

"Yet here you sit like a man who has nothing left." They both looked beyond the trees to the men there, enjoying themselves as they should. "The child of his father, Jake's father, will be like you should she live. The blood of the great-grandfather runs almost pure in the child."

"You think I don't know that? What would you have me do? Steal the child away? Raise it in darkness such as I live? I cannot take a child any more than.... Is this your favor? That I have myself a child?" He shook his head and looked to the trees again. Quincey did as well. "Bring it here?"

"It is a girl child, this child of the man. She will be born soon, in a fortnight, and when she is, there will be no one to take her in. She will be just different enough that she will never know love. Not happiness, nor will she be cared for in a manner that she should be." He turned in his seat and spoke low. "This child will need her brother. He will help her in ways that neither of us can. I wish...my favor of you is to ask them to take this child and care for her. If they should do this, I will grant them a gift of riches."

"They'll not want it. They'll say they have enough. That they need no more. These men, they are much like Jenna. One of blood, the other of love." He nodded at him. "You will offer them the gift of life. Immortality. The daughter will have it, they should as well."

"Agreed. And you will talk to them for me? Then retrieve the child before harm comes to her?" He said that he would. "I owe you, Quincey. More now than before."

"You are a sly man; I wish I had never met you." When he threw back his head and laughed, Quincey joined him. He was a good friend, after all. "I shall talk to them in the morning. They are having entirely too much fun at the moment for me to talk such seriousness now."

"I will leave it to you. But the child, she doesn't have much longer. There are forces that even now come for her." He nodded. Quincey had no idea what they were, but he knew if this man said so, then it was true. "I will talk to you after you speak with them. It will be then that I give you the information to save her."

Quincey sat there for a long while after his sire left him. He thought of the child that would need these men, and wondered if they would take her. Jake might be hesitant about it, but he thought Forrest would be the hardest to convince. He would know, too, that the child was a vampire. Quincey would also have to remove the spell on young Jake soon.

"What am I to do, Jenna? They will hate me for what I have kept from even you." He wondered too what she'd say if she had any idea that he'd been her father. That her mother had been the love of his life, and he'd not known about their child. "I should have told you. It was my plan to, but by the time I found you, you were too set in your ways to allow me to change you. I should have anyway."

When the couple came out of the woods, their bodies slick with sweat, he smiled as he pulled the shadows around him. He loved these men, like a man would a son, he supposed. As they got closer to the house, he listened to their words, their body language telling him more than their simple statements did. They were in love. The two of them were deeply in love.

"The office is going to be closed for the rest of the week. I thought we'd take a trip." Quincey wondered if he could guide them to the child, perhaps. But before he could suggest that to them, Forrest continued. "And I think you're right about the house. Selling it would be the best thing. Too many bad memories. I like your idea about Jenna's house."

"She left it to us both." Quincey had known that as well, and wondered if she'd told them that he lived in the sublevels. When Jake paused and looked right at him, he wondered if the man was already shedding his magic. "Do you feel that?"

Forrest stood next to Jake, protecting him as they both looked around. Quincey assured them with a touch of his mind to theirs that things were all right, to go in the house. When they did as he suggested, he made his way to his home.

Life for the two of them was about to get very busy. And for the first time in a while, Quincey knew that this was just what he needed. Smiling, he made his way to the lower levels and wondered what his life was going to be like as well.

Before You Go...

HELP AN AUTHOR

write a review

THANK YOU!

Share your voice and help guide other readers to these wonderful books. Even if it's only a line or two your reviews help readers discover the author's books so they can continue creating stories that you'll love. Login to your favorite retailer and leave a review. Thank you.

AWARD WINNING, BESTSELLING AUTHOR

Kathi Barton, author of the bestselling series Force of Nature, lives in Nashport, Ohio with her husband Paul. In addition to writing full time Kathi likes to spend time with her eight grandkids, three children and three children-in-laws. She writes to relax and have fun.

Her muse, a cross between Jimmy Stewart and Hugh Jackman, brings them to life for her readers in a way that has them coming back time and again for more. Her favorite genre is paranormal romance with a great deal of spice. You can visit Kathi online and drop her an email if you'd like. She loves hearing from her fans. aaronskiss@gmail.com.

Follow Kathi on her blog: http://kathisbartonauthor.blogspot.com/